'I really think it's a fine piece of sustained writing. The narrative drive is so very powerful I read it at one sitting. I think the subject is really powerful and powerfully expressed.'

Joan Bakewell

The Ladder

Michael Waterhouse

The Ladder

Published by The Conrad Press Ltd. in the United Kingdom 2022

Tel: +44(0)1227 472 874

www.theconradpress.com

info@theconradpress.com

ISBN 978-1-915494-27-6

Typesetting and Cover Design by: Charlotte Mouncey, www.bookstyle.co.uk

The Conrad Press logo was designed by Maria Priestley.

Printed and bound in Great Britain by Clays Ltd, Elcograf S.p.A

In memory of Margaret Elinor Waterhouse
(1927-1993)

PART ONE

1

GARY

October 2018

I looked in the mirror this morning and saw only blood.

The mirror is a small, square sheet of glass framed in pale blue wood. It hangs on the wall of my bathroom, above the basin and next to a print of Dali, which isn't mine.

How long do we ever look at ourselves in a mirror? A few seconds before leaving the house? Longer when shaving, except that, even then, I don't examine my whole face, just that part of my cheek or chin the razor grazes across. Then I look down to rinse the blade in soapy water.

This was different. I must have stood there for a full five minutes.

I saw blood, suffusing my face. Is that the phrase? It mottled and purpled my cheeks. It threaded the veins of my nose. There was an easy explanation, of course. Drink. Too much of it. But that wouldn't do. It wasn't a satisfactory answer. This face was more like evidence. What I saw had an irresistible truth about it. Here, reflected in the mirror, was my record.

And there was another, equally telling truth. Although I didn't like what I saw, I felt scarcely no guilt, nor even blame. So, what was it that I did feel, scrutinising this face I scarcely recognized as my own? Was I unsettled by him, embarrassed for him? I suspect that working inside me was some deep, ancestral canon, a universal conscience struggling to remind me that there are acceptable deeds and deeds that go beyond the pale. Does it have a voice, this canon, a voice in the mirror, saying 'You have transgressed'?

Possibly.

I spent the morning, or a couple of hours of it, lazing on a warm rock overlooking the ocean. High, white clouds were skittering across the bay. Between them, clear of cloud, when light splashed on the rock, I felt the sun's warmth land gently on my face and hands. It was like a blessing, a sanctifying touch, welcome in October, welcome after the last two years.

The rock rises in a steep cliff behind my house. I rented this place for its position. From the window seat in the sitting room, I have a commanding view across the bay and down the track that leads to the village. The track is the only way you can approach in a vehicle. On foot, you could climb up above the house and descend to it from the rock, but it's precipitous and you'd have to take it carefully and I'd have a good chance of seeing you from the kitchen or the bathroom. All in all, I'd be unlucky not to spot visitors.

I've been here for seven weeks now. In that time, there might have been half a dozen cyclists who have passed through, a few more hikers perhaps. I greet them in a friendly manner and show them where the old footpath continues beyond the rock. They seem appreciative, take me for a local.

The only regular I see is Angus. He runs the stores in the village and brings the post. He knows me as Greg. Greg Montrose. There's never any mail for me by name. Most of the stuff Angus pushes through my door is either for the owner of the house, or fliers. I haven't met the owner yet. He doesn't live on the island and we arranged my tenancy by email. Angus seems to think he keeps his distance. That suits me. The fewer people who know me, the better.

The island isn't large, maybe two hundred square miles. Those of us who live here are scattered about. I'll run into people if I'm in the village, but I quite often don't see anyone for days at a time. I suppose I'm used to remote places. When we were married, Kim and I would take short B&B holidays in the Highlands, her idea. She loved to be on the hill, trampling heather and dragging her boots through oily bogs. I did too, the tough climbs, the tart winds, but back then I also enjoyed the pub in the evenings, for the *craic* you understand, the company of others.

If I turn to face the sun, I can feel the warmth of it on my eyelids.

Now, of course, remoteness is what's required. I crave it.

On a clear day, I can see right across the bay to the Isles. I'm told whales visit this part of the coast in summer. God knows whether I'll be around then. It would be exciting.

We'll see.

2

After the G.P. left, I decided it was too late to do anything further that evening. Kim looked quite tranquil in her bed, an expression I'd not seen in over a year. I sat by her for a while, holding her limp hand in mine. Her fingernails were long, painted bright purple, the colour of new heather. I'd thought about cutting them only a few days earlier, but I was never much skilled at it and then there didn't seem much point.

When I'd imagined this day, as I had countless times, I'd always thought it would be extremely anguished. I'd expected to be in tears, in despair about the future and how I would survive it. But there was none of that. Instead, for a few hours, I had a sense of completion, the fulfilment of a plan, one drawn up a long time ago and likely to be months in the execution.

Had she had any idea? I think it's possible, but there's no way of knowing.

The following morning a firm of undertakers came to take her away. The men from Burrell & Cox were very efficient, I must say. They asked to see the death certificate, commiserated with me and then explained that although they were removing the body to their premises in the high street, I must feel free to call in at any time that they were open, should I want to view the body again. I hadn't begun to think of Kim as 'the body', but now that that was how she was to be referred to, she immediately seemed more distant from me, as if she were passing on. I told them that it was unlikely I'd visit.

'As you wish,' the man from Burrell & Cox said, and he handed me the wedding ring from Kim's finger.

I was exhausted. The last ten days had been an anxious time of preparation, and I'd struggled to sleep. Kim, too, had been restless. I wasn't at all sure why, but she seemed to sense that something was about to happen, and it made her agitated. Although she wasn't able to tell me what bothered her, and her capacity to show distress was, in any case, very limited by then, I knew. I could see it in her eyes. She was frightened. I suspected she was frightened of me, frightened of what I might do.

On the day, though, she was tranquil as a cat in sunshine.

Afterwards, I needed fresh air. The room was stifling. I stood in the porch and watched rush hour cars slide by.

Later, I tried to sleep, but it was no good. The sense of contentment I'd felt was slipping away. I was beginning to feel on edge. I was overwhelmed by the idea that I should be taking decisions, actions. But there was, in truth, nothing urgent to do. Peter Bruce, the GP, had mentioned that he needed to talk to me about something, but it could wait twenty-four hours he said. Even the funeral arrangements were already largely made. It would be a small affair. Kim had one living relative, a sister in Australia. I sat at my desk and emailed her an invitation, knowing she wouldn't come. She replied in three lines, sympathetic, but acknowledging that she and Kim hadn't been close in recent years. My immediate thought was: *and some*!

There was a woman called Sally I was aware of, vaguely - Kim had mentioned that they'd cycled together a few times – but I couldn't find a number or email for her.

She'd also had a friend down the road, Penny. At one time, they'd been best friends, went to the local multiplex together, the occasional drink. But all that had lapsed as Kim declined. I'd tried to avoid Penny. It seemed to me that all she did when we met was cry. If I bumped into her, she invariably said 'It's such a shame'.

Shame! What a wholly inadequate, shallow word. A belittling, tepid word, the kind of word suited to a weekend away when it rained the whole time.

I used to smile at Penny and say nothing.

Idly, I opened Kim's wardrobe. Most of her clothes hadn't been worn for months. I slid the jumpers and trousers, the dresses and tops, one by one, along the rail. Was I hoping to find something, a brightly coloured shirt that summed her up, a fleece that took me back a few years to a broken country stile, a track winding up a snowy mountain, to the era *before*? But they were all the same, her old clothes, discarded, mute, without a message.

She had a beautiful body, I think. That stays. That's indelible. Although she was athletic and strong, her shoulders were particularly slender and graceful. When she was naked, when she stepped out of the shower, I liked to tiptoe up behind her and place the lightest of kisses on her soft, damp skin, on her neck and shoulders, behind her ears. She'd more often than not shudder, surprised I was there, but then she'd turn her head slowly to one side, and that was my signal to carry on, kisses that were the touch of a feather, tender, quickly gone.

3

I climb down from the rock at what I guess is about lunchtime. I've nothing much in the house, just a few slices of bread and a block of cheddar. There might be beer in the fridge.

I hadn't anticipated the lengthy postscript I'm going through, in which Kim continues, in which I converse with her on a daily basis, perhaps three or four times. She's still with me.

The descent is difficult. The footholds that are easily found on the way up are obscured going down by overhangs and plants growing out of the cliff. They sway and flutter in the light breeze. I take my time. What have I got to hurry for? My feet search out clefts and ledges, and gradually I reach the knoll immediately behind the cottage.

From here, he's obvious. He stands out in his yellow oilskin jacket, as if he wants to be unmistakable in our brown landscape, *follais*, as the Scots say up here.

'Hello there!'

He turns, a blaze of sunflower, a grey bearded man, weathered. As he moves towards me, I notice his thick hands.

'Hello to you, Mr Montrose. We haven't met. My name is Struan Lamont. I fish off the machair down there.'

'Pleased to meet you, Mr Lamont.'

'And I you, Mr Montrose.'

I'm wondering what he wants, why he repeats my name, as

if he's testing its authenticity. He shakes my hand vigorously, then steps back, appraising. When he smiles, there are gaps in his teeth.

'I'd have called before,' he says, 'but there are always reasons for postponing, aren't there?'

'Of course. No matter.'

'You're settled in, then?'

'Yes. I think so. Takes a while, doesn't it? To get to know people and so on.'

'It certainly does here. We're not always as friendly as we might be.'

'Oh no, I wouldn't-- '

He waves me away, not interested in discussing the point. He knows his people. He knows their strengths and weaknesses. I don't think he minds that the local community is not particularly welcoming. He simply acknowledges it.

'Do you fish, Mr Montrose?'

'I have done.' I'm hesitating, not sure where we're headed. 'A little.'

'Well, now's your opportunity. A few of us are out on the boat this Saturday. Would you care to join us?'

'That would be….' I'm uncertain. 'Very kind.'

'You'd be doing us a favour, if I'm honest with you. I like to make up the numbers, and one of our lads has gone down with the flu.'

He laughs. More gaps emerge.

'This time of year,' he adds. 'He never fails.'

The flu amuses him. It must be this lad's propensity to go down with it every winter. Struan's laughter distances him. He's not susceptible to the flu himself, I'm guessing.

'What time?' I ask.

'We'll need to catch the tide, of course. It's late on Saturday. Shall we say 7.30 on the quay?'

'I'll be there.'

'I'm sure you will, Mr Montrose. Good day to you. Wrap up warm, won't you?'

'I will. Thank you.'

Struan Lamont walks quickly. He's out of the gate and down the hill before I've entered my key in the latch.

4

She fell in the woods. That was the start. It had been raining and the path was wet underfoot. Where it climbed, it was churned up by boots and dogs. At least one bicycle had been through. I found it difficult to keep upright myself. Each step I took I felt my feet slide beneath me. I called out behind 'You alright?' and she was. Kim was strong, a hill walker, not easily deterred by bad weather or slippery conditions.

'Deer,' I said.

We stopped to examine the tracks: two exclamation marks picked out in the mud, probably left there just as the light came up. There was a point where the two tracks stood parallel.

'It's come to a halt,' Kim said. 'It's looking around.'

'Taking in the landscape.'

'Do you think it's frightened?'

'Maybe. A young one, you think?'

'I can't tell. I'm not enough of an expert. Are the tracks of a young deer different from old ones?'

'I believe so.'

We moved on, picturing a young deer walking through the wood, its head jerking backwards every footfall, pausing, a hind leg half raised, scenting the air, gently stretching its ears, then sudden flight. Off!

'They have such power,' she said. 'You remember my parents

had a little dog? Sanky? I took her for a walk in Richmond Park once, and I don't think we were particularly near the deer, but it was the time of year when the does are very protective of their young. Anyway, one of them came up to us and it was obvious to me that the deer didn't like having Sanky around, and I knew that one kick from her and Sanky would be a goner. So I tried pushing the doe away. You've never felt such a wall of hard muscle. She would not budge.'

'What did you do?'

'I picked up Sanky and ran for it, and the deer came after us. Just for twenty yards or so. But I have to say it scared the life out of me.'

'I'm not surprised. How was poor Sanky?'

'I think she was sublimely oblivious to the whole thing. I don't think she even realised she was in danger.'

Then she fell.

We were back in single file, and I was ahead, shifting through heavy, wet, autumn leaves. She called out my name as she went down, and I turned. She'd slipped and fallen backwards, and was lying with her back against the trunk of an oak, her legs splayed out in front of her. She made no effort to get up.

I hurried over and knelt down to her. There was something not quite right. She'd fallen awkwardly and had clearly struck the tree with some force, but I couldn't account for her not trying to pull herself up.

'I don't think I can, darling. I can't make my legs work.'

There was anxiety in her face, a look I'd come to recognize over the years, when we were about to board a plane, when a frozen pipe burst, when we knew Adrianna was likely to die. She was afraid that something permanent had happened.

I thought of the phrase *life changing injuries,* the expression broadcasters employ after the latest knife outrage.

'Come on, let's get you on your feet.'

I squeezed in between the trunk and her back, and grabbed her under her arms, pulled her up. For a moment, I thought she'd collapse again, but her legs held and after a few reassuring words from me, she took a couple of steps and decided she was fine, recovered.

'That was peculiar,' she said.

'You slipped in the mud. Nothing peculiar about that. I've nearly gone over several times.'

'No, I don't mean the fall. I mean how I felt when I was lying there.'

'Forget about it.'

I think she did, although I can't be sure. There were other occasions, other symptoms. Perhaps this registered as the first, I don't know. When it started to matter, she didn't dwell on the causes, the premonitions.

We remember the good times, don't we?

Yes, my darling. We do.

5

There are some days when the wind bites at my front door, like it would break it down. The windows are ineptly sealed, letting in the cold where the sashes fasten. As I go to tighten the latches, I can feel chill air on the palms of my hands. In our old house, we always imagined the building to be a bastion that held weather at bay. Here, I sense that houses, outside and in, experience the elements, participate in them. They have permeable borders.

There's no central heating, but I keep the wood burner stacked. One innovation I've introduced is that a green curtain, velvet, now hangs inside the front door. It keeps out the worst of the wind. Otherwise, when the days are cold, I resort to another jumper. Last week, on a really bitter night, I sat at the kitchen table in the navy woollen jacket I bought in the Selfridge's sale and watched my breath curl away from me.

That seems like a long time ago.

The phone rings. Every time it does, I'm shocked. I've persuaded myself that no one knows that I'm here, no one knows my phone number, but of course the locals do, and occasionally someone from the village will ring, usually to sell me something. Do you need another delivery of logs? Would you be for having your windows cleaned, Mr Montrose?

I've taken to ignoring it when it rings, just in case the person at the other end isn't local. Can I lead my life like this, afraid to answer the phone, convinced that the villagers are about to unmask me, viscerally scared that the world I once knew is making its slow, dogged way to my doorstep?

I've decided to brave the village again. Bravery comes into it only because, over the last seven weeks, I've tried to avoid any more than essential contact with the village and the villagers. Effectively, I've been a recluse. But I realise now that I'm in danger of arousing suspicion. If I'm seen to be keeping to myself too much, people may begin to think that I have secrets. God forbid, they might even start snooping about! Far better that they see enough of me to become indifferent, to lose interest in me. I need to be adequately friendly. Accepting Struan Lamont's invitation to go fishing is a step in that direction.

I take the track that leads down to the village. It's probably about a mile and a half to the general stores and post office, one of a number of buildings that greet you as you enter the village street. I realise now why I've been so reluctant to go out. As soon as I reach the post office, I feel all eyes are on me. I swear people are lifting their curtains and peering at me, binoculars raised, fingers dialling me into focus. They see me sharply, closely, a man who has stayed here for nearly two months, much longer than any of the holidaymakers they are used to. What does he want here? Where has he come from? How long does he plan to remain on the island?

Do they know that I've taken a six-month lease on the cottage?

Angus greets me as I step into his store.

'If you're here,' he says, 'you might as well take your post.'

'I should think you can throw it away, Angus. It's only fliers, isn't it?'

'That's as may be, Mr Montrose. But we don't *throw away* in these parts. We are recyclers!'

'Oh well, recycle away.'

I'm irritated by his self-righteousness.

The store is empty. I am its only customer. It endeavours to provide anything the villagers could possibly need. As well as newspapers and food supplies, Angus has rope, motor oil, candles, a collection of magazines and paperback books, disposable nappies, footballs in four different shiny colours, oilskins, gloves, shovels, hammers, electric drills, paint for exteriors and paint for interiors, medicines, hair dye, duvets and garden benches. He will order a dishwasher or fridge for you and have it delivered to your house within three or four days. Behind his counter, he has four shelves of alcohol, a bottle of anything you fancy.

'Did you have any postal requirements yourself, Mr Montrose? A package to send perhaps?'

He makes a move towards the glass panelled office that occupies one corner of the store.

'Do you not need to communicate with the mainland?'

'Not at the moment,' I reply, and I thank him for his interest.

'Where exactly is it that you're from?'

Angus leans forward on his counter. He has the look of a man expecting a revelation. I'm sorry to disappoint him.

'Oh, right down south, Angus. A long way from here.'

'Are we talking in the vicinity of London, then?'

'There or thereabouts.'

'You're a secretive man, Mr Montrose.'

He bends down behind the counter and fetches up a large

hessian sack of potatoes.

'What sort of weight were you after?'

'If you could give me eight, that would do.' I'm conscious that he still awaits an answer about my origins. I must make something up. 'I don't mean to be secretive, Angus. It's just that where I come from, near Croydon, is just another outer London suburb. It's not desperately interesting. It has none of the beauty you have on the island.'

Angus counts out eight potatoes. He places them carefully, one by one, each encrusted with dark soil, into a brown paper bag.

'Does it have a name this "not desperately interesting" place?'

'Sanderstead.'

'Sanderstead?' He twists the two open corners of the bag and swings it in his hands, twice, in full circles, fastening the bag closed. 'I hope you're not thinking we're overly nosey here in the village. We like to know our kith.'

'Of course, and I don't suppose the residents change much over the years.'

'They don't. People have children. The elderly go. We're quite content with that.'

He pushes the bag across the counter. There is a finality about it that seems, in some elliptical way, to settle the unvarying life of the village he describes.

'I'll just help myself to bread and eggs,' I tell him.

It's a relief to step away from the counter, but I feel his eyes following me as I walk around. I am making a fool of myself and he is happy to watch. I have no idea where to look. His patience bores into me.

'Bread and eggs, you say?'

'Aye.'

I've said it without meaning to. It strikes a false note, an Englishman pretending, but I've heard the word so often in recent weeks it's hard not to imitate.

'They'll be behind you,' Angus explains.

They sit together at eye level on the same shelf, boxes of eggs and plastic bags of sliced bread.

'Do you have a living, Mr Montrose?'

'Used to.'

I carry the bread and eggs to Angus's counter.

'What was it you did?'

I must think of something convincing, something I seem to fit and which I'll find easy to remember the next time I'm asked. I mustn't give myself skills that I might be called upon to use. I can't be an osteopath or an electrician.

'I was the manager of a small estate agency.'

'Property! There's good money in that.'

'Not much of it came my way, I can assure you.'

'So you were not a very good estate agent?'

'No, I did a fair enough job.'

Why do I bother to reply? Why should I care about my success in a career I've invented for myself? I suppose my pride is injured. It's a weakness I should guard against. If I start arguing with people about my made-up past, I risk coming risibly unstuck. After all, apart from the obvious, I know very little about the day-to-day working life of an estate agent. I may tie myself up in knots.

'But you're probably right, Angus.'

'Aach, you disappoint me. You shouldn't agree with my cavils. My wife says I'm addicted to mischief. She's amazed folk come near this shop.'

'We couldn't do without you, Angus.'

I decide it's time to go. I pay up and sort my shopping into a rucksack I brought for the purpose. He watches me pack away the items.

'As an estate agent, you might have found yourself a better place to live.'

Another of Angus's cavils?

'And why is that? It suits me well enough.'

I'm interested to know what failings he believes the cottage has.

'Have you not discovered for yourself? I'm assuming not. It leaks. The cottage leaks. If we get the snow or the heavy rain, it finds its way in. Have you not seen the damp sitting in the walls? You'd better pray for a dry winter up there.'

'I shall.'

'I'll lay in extra buckets for you.'

'I suppose I could contact the owner and suggest a few repairs.'

'Good luck to you there. I haven't seen him on the island in ten years. He hated the place when he lived up there and, once he'd left, he could see no good reason to return.'

'Why doesn't he sell up?'

'The question we all ask ourselves. No idea.'

'I might drop him a line all the same.'

'Aye, you do that.'

I have my rucksack on my shoulder. There is nothing further to say. The odd thought occurs to me that Angus is giving me permission to leave.

6

The time *before* seems like a different era, as distant as childhood to the adult of sixty or appeasement to the warrior of '44. The time when I worked, when I had a full-time job, has been similarly absorbed by history. I stopped going to the office to care for Kim just a matter of months ago, but it has the haziness of years, a chasm apart.

It turned out to be straightforward to transport my work to our bedroom. As a travel writer, more of an editor by then, certainly not an estate agent, all I required was a laptop and my mobile. An imaginative guy at the office called Saul updated my software and that enabled me to include photos and rudimentary graphics in the articles I was preparing for the guide. It was easy work, interruptible when Kim needed me.

There was a time when I was the one who backpacked in the Andes, swam fjords in western Norway, even motorcycled in Jordan. It was my accounts of hotels, government hostels, sleeping rough, that appeared in the guides to those destinations. People went travelling with me in their jacket pockets, heeded my advice on what and what not to eat, local beers and wines, the dodgy districts of major cities, the vistas and wildlife that shouldn't be missed.

Then I turned thirty. Kim wasn't as patient about my going away as she had been, and when I was offered the chance of a desk job, editing other reporters' material, I accepted. I accepted it rather than grabbed it, and with reluctance, I should add. There were many days when I sat down to work with itchy feet and a yearning for uncertainty.

So long ago, Kim, at least nostalgically, how it lies in the gut.

Of course, by the end, work had reduced to an hour or so after she'd gone to sleep.

Some days I did none.

7

The mountain turned to beaten copper in the late afternoon light. Kim's skin glowed, and she could scarcely keep her eyes open, it was so bright.

We'd taken the cable car. I'd had to persuade her with a glass of white wine to settle her nerves. When we stepped out of the bar and she took in the steep incline the car would travel up to reach the top, I thought she might baulk, but she went ahead and took her seat on the bench and smiled up at me.

'I don't know where this comes from,' she said.

'Your fear of heights?'

'I love climbing mountains, but something like this!'

The car jolted and she covered her mouth to suppress the urge to scream. We started to ascend. As we rose up the mountain and the coastline began to open out, she relaxed.

We'd decided to visit Table Mountain at sunset because people we'd met wouldn't stop talking about the colours that fill the sky as the sun disappears. That moment was still to come. For now, what we could see was a scattering of grey clouds that hung like smoke, black tankers just visible on the horizon, a confused welter of rock dropping away beneath the cable car.

We'd brought wine, strictly illegal on the mountain, but the thing to do we'd been told, just as the sun begins to be swallowed up. The corkscrew I'd remembered at the last minute pressed uncomfortably against my hip.

We stepped out at the top. There were others with bottles and plastic glasses, twenty or so of us, all with the same plan. We'd struggle to find a spot with a good view and no neighbours. I took Kim's hand and we walked a bit faster.

'I hope this isn't going to be a disappointment,' she said.

'Why should it be?'

'The whales?'

'That was simply ignorance.'

Hermanus. Three days earlier. We'd slogged up the N2 in a hire car, and positioned ourselves in Walker Bay, exactly where we'd been advised to, and waited. We must have stayed there for a couple of hours, watching an unbroken ocean. I took a stroll around and spoke to two locals, who told me we were wasting our time and to come back in September or October. That's when to catch them.

'We lost several hours of valuable sun-bathing,' Kim said, as we turned the car around and headed back.

The evening sun was dropping. We chose a rock with a ledge that looked as if it had been worn smooth by sunset worshippers. Kim sat down and I uncorked the wine and handed her a glass.

'It's just so beautiful,' she said. 'Robben Island?'

She was pointing, unsure in the brilliant light.

'That's it. Shaped like a liver.'

'We must go there.'

'Absolutely. I think you have to book up several days in advance.'

'We can do that.'

'Sure.'

It had been one of those easy, lazy days, when we'd done very little before setting off for the mountain. We'd had lunch at a fish restaurant in Simon's Town. We both had Shad, beautifully fresh. We were enjoying ourselves, half-way through our holiday, the weather perfect. Apart from the Hermanus whales, everything was living up to expectations.

'Do you ever worry about the future?'

She turned away from the sun and, after the brightness of the bay, I couldn't see how serious she was.

'Money, do you mean? Not having enough?'

'No, not money. Do you ever wonder whether things will work out for us? In the long run?'

She sipped from her glass and then placed it on the ledge. I pulled out my phone and took a photo of her.

'We've done pretty well so far,' I said.

And we had. Eighteen years, to be exact. I felt our love was as strong as it had been at the beginning. It was true that we'd been tested, especially when we lost Adrianna, and we would never entirely recover from that. But our marriage had survived it, and we'd come through the subsequent distress of not being able to conceive again. We'd talked about adoption, and without either of us voicing the decision, didn't pursue it. After all that, to be able to stand here and know that, at no point, did we not want to be together, must be a sign of the strength of the relationship. I felt sure.

A light breeze lifted the hem of her dress. The white cotton set off the tan of her legs.

'I'm sometimes paralysed by fear,' she said. 'I'm frightened something will go wrong and all this, this lovely life, will fall apart and we'll struggle to believe we ever had it.'

'What's brought this on?'

'I don't know. Too much pleasure perhaps. Too much privilege.'

'Well, don't let it spoil the moment, my love.'

'No, of course. I'm sorry. I'm being silly.'

The whole sky sat refracted, colours sprayed across it, a panorama of yellow, pink and indigo, and strings of white floss. Our outcrop of rock went dark and there was a chill in the air. Kim stood up and I hugged her to me as we took in the view.

'Gorgeous!'

Her mood had improved, deflected like the scattered light above us.

'Shall we head back?' I asked.

'Just a little longer,' she said, and nuzzled into me.

All that remained of the sun was a burning rim of molten red far out at sea. It was growing cold, but we must have stood there for twenty minutes, gripped, reluctant to give up the beauty.

I still have the photographs from that trip to South Africa. There's one of Kim I particularly love. She is in her white, strapless dress, with the pleated front and a skirt that stopped just above her knees. It was the only item that finally meant something when I was sorting out her wardrobe. She is happy, tanned, exultant. The photo was taken in Hermanus, I believe, before we realised what a futile visit it had been. I'd like to display it, on the mantelpiece or the pinboard I have above the microwave in the kitchen, but it's too risky. If I were to have visitors who, by some chance, gained access, came into the house, there'd be bound to be questions about her.

'Your wife, Mr Montrose? She's very pretty.'

Then there'd be more probing about her name, where she is,

why she isn't with me, and I'd have to invent another life for her, lie about her. I couldn't bear it. It would dishonour her memory, sully her. I know there will eventually come a time when I'll have to explain why I'm here on my own, but for now I'd rather they didn't know about Kim, not yet.

'You must miss her, Mr Montrose.'

Why is it they keep repeating my name, as if they don't quite believe it? It's common enough. I chose it because I thought it was the kind of name they'd have heard of in these parts.

In my naiveté, I'd anticipated that it would be easy to live a solitary life here. I'd remembered the island as sparsely populated and remote, the kind of destination people came to on retreat. It had never occurred to me that I would be an object of curiosity, to be resolved and categorised. We all have to fit, though, don't we? Even if it's an awkward fit.

Now that I'm under scrutiny, I have to be mindful of anything that might not accord with the image I've given myself, the image of Greg Montrose, former estate agent from south Croydon. Do the books I have, the music I listen to, seem anachronistic? Would Greg read travel writers like Freya Stark and Norman Lewis, listen to Sibelius and Miles Davis? Why not? Why can't Greg enjoy reading and listening to whatever he damn well pleases?

8

I was on the quay promptly at 7.30 on Saturday morning. It was just after dawn, the sky pale pink, hints of sunlight on the snowcaps of the mountains. I felt exhilarated in a way I hadn't done for months.

The short quay was stacked high with lobster pots. Alongside them, racks of dried fishing nets smelt like cheap paint. I guessed that was some kind of preservative.

I made my way down the broad wooden boarding towards Struan Lamont's trawler. He was helping two men in oilskins to board. Their tentative movements made me think they hadn't been on many boats before. Struan Lamont handed them down onto the deck and grabbed their fishing rods from the quay. They looked brand new.

Three other fishing boats were tied up in the small harbour, but our trawler appeared to be the only vessel planning to go out that morning.

'Mr Montrose, you are welcome!'

Struan Lamont leant forward and extended a hand to me.

Well, what do we make of this, Kim?

I took his hand and pulled myself over the gunwale. The deck ran most of the length of the boat. To the fore, lobster pots and bait bags piled up against the wheelhouse. Inside, two men in wide-legged yellow waders were smoking and drinking tea. I nodded in their direction and one of them waved back with his roll-up.

'Any chance of a cuppa, Struan?'

'You have only to ask, sir. Have a word with Iain in the cabin there.'

I watched him hoick a crate of beer bottles off the quay.

'Do you need a hand?' I asked.

'No, I'll be fine.'

'What are we after today?'

'Pollock and mackerel, mainly.'

'You've no lobsters to pick up then?

'Not this time of year, Mr Montrose. You'll have to wait for the summer months for that kind of treat.'

He span away from me and carried the beer down to the stern.

We were eight on board. Struan had two crew. The two novices turned out to be Germans, on vacation in the Highlands, and there were a couple of islanders like me, whom I'd seen about in the village, but never talked to. I went over to the wheelhouse in search of tea.

'Could you do me a cuppa, please,' I asked Iain.

He snapped out his cigarette on the chart table and picked up the kettle.

'You live in that cottage up on the hill?' he said.

'That's right. Moved in a few weeks ago.'

'How do you find the island? Like it?'

'I do.'

'Bit different from what you're used to, I imagine.'

'Certainly is.'

'Down south, I mean.'

'Word gets round.'

'You sneeze in that cottage and they'll be blessing you in the pub.'

The trawler's motor purred as it nudged the quay. Struan was unwinding mooring rope from the capstan and coiling it onto the deck. Once he'd cast off, he came forward to the wheelhouse, geared the engine and we started to head out.

The air was cold and sharp, a briny edge to it. Beyond the harbour, the sea was slate grey and lumpy. I struggled a little to keep my balance, and when Iain handed me a mug, the tea slopped on my hand, scalding me. I don't think he was even aware he'd done it.

'How far are we going?' I asked Struan.

'Mile. Mile and a half. Weather forecast is none too good, and I don't want my paying customers all wet and growling. There's plenty of fish in this near water.'

I stepped out on deck. I was glad I'd accepted Struan's invitation. I didn't much care whether I landed any fish, but to be out on a boat in the early morning, a chapping wind on my face, rackety seagulls sweeping around us, was invigorating.

I told Kim. She laughed. *You hate mackerel!*

We anchored off a bay to the north of the island. It wasn't a place I knew. I gathered from Struan that, for generations, islanders had largely avoided the north. They'd ceased to build there or farm the land. There were still a handful of broken-down houses, widely scattered, and the coastal rocks were occupied by seals and gannets and oystercatchers. Occasionally, birdwatchers strayed up there, but otherwise it was deserted.

I watched the hard coastline. A seal slunk lazily into a wave and two others raised their heads, curious as we came into view. I thought I felt rain in the air.

Struan Lamont distributed rods to those of us who hadn't brought our own and we took up positions around the deck. I'd fished on the open sea maybe only half a dozen times before, but I remembered how to cast. I flipped the lever to free up the spool, leaned the rod back and spun out the line. The sea was so choppy it was difficult to be certain where it cut the water. I wedged myself up against the gunwale and waited.

The Germans were on my left, chatting to each other. I'd no idea what they were saying, but even without a word of their language, it was clear to me they were determined they would finish the morning with a catch. They threw their lines angrily. They were impatient for the fish to bite and reeled in too soon. When Struan Lamont realised what they were doing, he went over to give them advice.

The rain increased. I was sure it was only a shower.

I cast again and waited for my line to tauten.

I travelled up here on a whim. I knew I wanted somewhere remote, and inhospitable enough not to encourage visitors, but it could have been anywhere. I spent a few weeks in Norway, a place far to the north. Gibraltar, too. In the end, Scotland made sense because I knew parts of it and I'd holidayed here on the island one time. I felt that in Scotland I would behave, if not naturally, then with sufficient familiarity that people would accept me, wouldn't raise their eyebrows.

I got that pretty comprehensively wrong.

'They're away in themselves.'

Struan had come up behind me, and I hadn't heard.

'The Germans?'

'Aye. Competing with each other. Competing with their own pride. They're always the same.'

'You're not a fan?'

'Their money's good. They can be as competitive as they like for as long as that's true.'

We'd fished for most of three hours when Struan informed us that he was cooking a breakfast of what we'd caught. I hadn't picked up much. A small pollock and seven or eight mackerel flapped, unappetisingly, at the bottom of my bucket. The Germans seemed alarmed at the thought that their hard-won catch might be redistributed amongst lesser fishermen. Struan assured them that there was plenty to go round and they would only be providing what they wanted to eat themselves.

The fish were quick fried on a couple of Primus stoves and Struan had boiled up some potatoes to go with them. We sat in light rain, picnic plates on our knees, and I felt this was the best day I'd had since arriving on the island. It had just gone twelve noon. The morning had been sharp and cold and wet, but the taste of that fresh pollock was unlike any fish I could remember. I'm sure the smell of the sea, taken in with every forkful, made a difference. The fish flaked and melted in my mouth.

'Will you be coming out again, Mr Montrose?'

I suddenly realised how absorbed I'd been in what I was eating, scarcely conscious of the people around me. My station was close to the wheelhouse. Iain was speaking to me over his shoulder while he concentrated on holding the boat steady.

'I hope so,' I said.

'We're out here pretty regular, you know. Struan usually has us on the water two or three times a week, maybe more.'

'Weather permitting?'

'Och, no. The weather's no bother. We come out in all sorts.

It has to be heavy to stop old Struan there. No, it's more the issue of whether he has the customers.'

Struan Lamont was raising the anchor, making ready for our return. The rain streamed down his beard and yellow oilskin jacket. He wore no gloves as he coiled the chain, his thick hands wet and red. He was used to it. This was how he earned his living. The cold and the wet meant nothing to him.

Iain gunned the engine and swung the trawler about. He steered round the headland and once the boat was heading for harbour, rolled himself a cigarette and took up with me again.

'This island would be a poor, backward place without Struan Lamont. I don't suppose you'd know, Mr Montrose.'

'No, no, I didn't,' I said. 'He's a sort of community leader, is he?'

'Aye, that's it. He's a strong sense of duty. To his fellow man – and woman.'

'Helps people out?'

'Definitely, but you wouldn't want to get on the wrong side of him.'

'No?'

'Your life wouldn't be worth living on this island.'

Iain laughed. He slurped his mug of tea noisily, as if it were part of his amusement.

'Does he have a wife?' I asked.

'Used to. She died.'

'I'm sorry to hear that.'

'Aye, well, it was a while ago. Cancer. Isn't it always? Forget which one now. It took years and years to work its way through her. She was a sorry sight by the end. Couldn't feed herself, go to the toilet. A sorry sight, I tell you.'

This took me aback. I hadn't expected it. I stumbled over my words.

'And eventually?'

'Eventually?'

Iain glanced quickly at me, surprised that I made so little sense. Then he took his eyes back to the sea.

'You said "eventually", Mr Montrose. What do you mean by that?'

I was finding it difficult to say. I felt I paused after each word I spoke.

'I meant that…eventually…she died of it, did she?… It was what you'd call….a natural death?'

'Oh aye, it killed her in the end.'

'I'm sorry to hear that.'

I had said that before. I was struggling.

'It destroyed one side of her body until there was nothing working well enough to keep her alive.'

'Terrible.'

'Long in the past, though. She couldn't have been more than fifty. He looked after her, Struan did, until her last days. He did everything for her. He watched her wither away, a bit weaker each month. Take my hat off to him. Not something we could all do, is it, Mr Montrose?'

'No, no, it isn't.'

I had to get away from him. I couldn't stand it, what he was saying. I strode up the deck to the stern. I needed the rain to wash my face, the sore wind to bite my cheeks, to feel pain.

Are you there? Speak to me, Kim. Are you there? Tell me the blood in my face, the blood I see in the mirror, tell me it isn't sin.

9

It was the morning after Kim's death, and I was in a state of anticipation that occupies many bereaved minds, I suspect, between the moment of loss and the funeral. I was convinced that something monumental was about to occur, little realising that that huge event had already happened.

I was conscious of the need not to make rash decisions. I was still in two minds about whether to sell our house or rent it out. Then, there was the shop to consider.

I received a call on my mobile from our GP, Dr Bruce. He'd indicated the day before that he had something he wanted to discuss with me, so I wasn't surprised to hear from him. But he sounded awkward on the phone, reluctant to get to the point.

'How are you, Gary?' he asked. 'How are you coping?'

'Oh, you know,' I said. What does one say in these situations? I'd just lost the woman I'd loved for over twenty years. It felt like a couple of hours ago. I thought he should know, a doctor with his experience, a better way to handle me.

'I thought I'd check to see how you are.'

'Yes,' I said. 'That's kind of you.'

'There's plenty of support out there for people in your situation. You don't have to deal with it alone.'

'No? Thank you.'

'There was another reason for ringing.'

Naturally. GPs, these days, don't have the time to make courtesy calls.

'Did Kim ever talk to you about organ donation?'

That came as a shock, not a conversation I'd expected.

'You do realise the funeral is on Wednesday?' I said.

'Yes.' He paused. 'I know that.'

'Won't that make it impossible? I mean, she's to be buried at St John's. In the churchyard. It's all arranged.'

'I'm sorry, Gary.' His voice suggested regret, recognition that he could have introduced the subject less abruptly. 'This must be upsetting news.'

'News?'

'Call. An upsetting call. I'm sure it would be better explained face to face, don't you think?'

I agreed to an appointment later that day, which gave me next to no time to consider what it was I should, or should not, agree to. Organ donation, so far as I could recall, was not something Kim and I had discussed. I wondered what had prompted Peter Bruce to approach me about it now, too late you might think, when there had been many earlier opportunities to raise it with Kim herself.

The idea was, of course, unsettling. I'd assumed the medical and legal issues were over. Peter Bruce had signed Kim's death certificate. I'd registered her death. I really did not want to delay the funeral. Kim would say that I was fretting unnecessarily, but then she did have a tendency to underestimate the scale of a problem.

Dr Bruce appeared at three promptly. I took him into the sitting room and offered him coffee or tea, which he declined.

'I won't keep you long.'

No? How could he be sure of that? Perhaps there was a formula to meetings like this. I sat opposite him and waited for him to start the conversation.

'There's never a good time to talk about dying and its consequences, is there?'

'I suppose not,' I said. 'Though Kim and I managed it often enough.'

'Really?'

I watched him shift his position and uncross his legs. He took out some paperwork from his backpack, uncapped his pen. I suspected that he had made little or no preparation for this meeting. It annoyed me.

'Gary,' he said. 'I'm loosely involved in a research project, based in Oxford, that's looking into degenerative conditions and what we can learn neurologically from donated tissues post-mortem.'

'Is neurology a particular interest of yours, then?'

'It is, yes. If I hadn't decided on general practice, that's what I would have done. I keep my hand in. I'm what they call a *gipsy*, a GP with a special interest.'

Why was he telling me this? Was I supposed to care about his research, admire it even?

I stood up and walked over to the sitting room window. The first leaves were just appearing, greening the trees in the March sunshine. A light breeze swayed the taller branches of the silver birches at the centre of the lawn. The day looked bright, expectant. I remembered how much Kim had loved the spring, its tangible prospect of change.

'What is it exactly you want my consent to?'

'We would like to remove Kim's brain and spinal cord.'

'We?' I asked.

'I would arrange the surgery and then the tissue would be placed in what's called the Oxford Brain Bank for later analysis.'

I continued to study the garden.

'Look, I don't begin to understand why this has come up now. Kim is dead. Why was this not discussed with her?'

'It was, Gary. It was her wish. She wrote to me and said that she would like to donate her organs, if they would be of any scientific use.'

'And would they be? Given what happened to her.'

'Yes, of course. But she failed to get around to completing the necessary forms.'

I was baffled. I had no memory of Kim mentioning the idea.

'Why wasn't I told about this?'

'She asked me not to say anything to you. I think she thought you would object.'

'Do I have any choice in the matter?'

'Of course. We need your consent before any surgery can be carried out. It wouldn't alter Kim's appearance, by the way.'

'The time to demand this was back then.'

'It's not a demand, Gary. As I say, we are seeking your permission.'

I was bluffing, of course, masking my true anxiety with indignation. I thought that if I came across as a widower upset and resentful at the suggestion that my wife's body should be cut open, Peter Bruce wouldn't spot my fear, the possibility that I might have something to hide.

'If I agree to this, what benefit will it have?'

He had it off pat.

'Hard to say. What we do know, so far, is that the work that's going on into studying the brain has made great strides in the understanding of things like autism and dementia.'

I went back to the sofa and sat down. Dr Bruce was waiting for my approval.

'When would it be done?'

'As soon as I can arrange it.'

'So I will have to delay the funeral?'

'No, that won't be necessary. The funeral arrangements can be left as they are.'

'But you need my agreement today?'

'If you're willing to give it, Gary, yes. I can provide you with the name of someone you can contact if you change your mind. You can withdraw your consent at any time over the next twenty-four hours.'

I was tempted to withhold consent there and then, to say to medical science that, if it were interested in learning more about Kim's disease, I should have been told earlier, that it had, consequently, missed the boat. But I knew that it wasn't that simple. For all Peter Bruce's politeness, his sympathetic manner, the impression he gave me that discretion lay with me and that I could refuse to cooperate, the implication of my refusal would undoubtedly be to arouse suspicion. The presumption, from the point of view of the GP surgery, must always be that if Kim had agreed, why ever should I object?

'I shan't keep you much longer,' he said. 'Can I take it that you are happy for us to go ahead?'

I nodded.

'I'm sorry, Gary. I do need you to say so.'

'Yes,' I said, peremptorily. 'You have my consent.'

'If you'd be kind enough to sign just there.'

He slid a form across the table and I scribbled my name where he'd indicated.

'Thank you,' he said.

He stood, felt unnecessarily for the phone in his jacket pocket, and offered me his hand. 'If you'd like to be kept informed about the research, that can be arranged. I'm afraid there may be a small fee.'

'Inevitably.'

'Nothing's free these days, eh?'

He swung his backpack on to his shoulder.

'Don't forget about bereavement support. It can help. They're good people.'

He showed himself out and, in that instant, I was aware of a powerful urge to flee. As soon as it was practical, perhaps in a few weeks, I must leave. I would have to make arrangements at the shop, and rent out the house, of course, but I could then get away. Instinctively, I thought I would need to give myself another name, find a place to live where I was unknown and likely to be untraceable.

I had to say my final goodbye to my life with Kim, and vanish.

10

KIM

8th November 2016 – two years earlier

I've begun to suspect that something isn't entirely right with me. I notice that when I go to open the shop in the mornings, I'm not as quick to insert the keys and turn the locks. It isn't significantly different, a matter of seconds, and I don't suppose, if Annie were watching me, she would pick up on it. But it's obvious to me. It's subtle, not as definable as a fumble or a slip, more a hint of awkwardness, as much in the mind as the fingers.

I'm not going to tell Gary. I'm sure it will pass or, if not, I'll take myself to the GP and have him sort it out. Gary needn't know. He'd only fret and make a fuss, and insist on us spending large amounts on private tests that aren't necessary. I want to shout at him sometimes. I know it's out of love for me, his deep care for my well-being, but the audible sighs are maddening.

'Good morning, Annie.'

Annie always looks pretty. She must be touching forty now, but she still has her figure and she dresses well. She buys expensive clothes in a classic style, simple lines and bold colours. I like her in red. She wears heels every day, even though we are on our feet, serving people, arranging and despatching orders, for eight hours, often more.

'What's on for today?' I ask.

She opens up the diary and flicks through to today's date. This morning she wears a vivid, rich burgundy varnish on her fingernails. She turns the pages neatly, light catching the red polish. She is very presentable, I think. It's partly why I hired her, over ten years ago now, when the business was just taking off. She made a difference. I've never asked any of them, but I believe a number of our customers, especially men, come to our shop because they want to be served by her.

She speaks well, too.

'Mr Armstrong is due in at eleven to collect his roses. We have a delivery to the BUPA home this afternoon, and I'm planning to make up a few sample bouquets for the window.'

'Good thinking.'

She stands at the workbench, severing the ends from Mr Armstrong's roses, trimming them to an equal length. I can't take my eyes off her burgundy nails and the yellow of the roses.

It all started with colour. The yellow roses remind me of the beer mat I scribbled the idea down on that night I was in the pub with Gary. It was a drunken joke really. Neither of us took it seriously for several weeks. I've always been fanatical about colour, about filling whatever environment I'm in with as much radiant colour as I can. What was it John Ruskin said? 'The purest and most thoughtful minds are those which love colours the most.' I felt flattered by that. *The Stones of Venice*, I think. You should see the paintings I have on my walls - prints of Mondrian, Van Gogh, Dufy - the shades I've chosen for our furnishings, the curtains, lampshades.

For me, back then before the pub, enjoying colour was just a hobby, something that brightened my week, my life. Every Monday I used to buy a few bunches of flowers, full of light, and take them home and distribute them around the house. I had my job in marketing, not thrilled with it and not the career I'd anticipated after graduating in French, for God's sake, but it was okay, paid the bills, and if you're holding down a dull day job, colours don't half lift your spirits when you get home at night. Healthier than a G & T.

But make them into a business? The idea of a shop dedicated to colour? Never crossed my mind.

Until that gin-soaked evening in The Green Man.

Am I deluding myself?

'Tea, Annie?'

'Please,' she says, but doesn't interrupt her work.

I pull myself away. Why am I so obsessed with colours? They rivet me and blind me to all other thoughts. I've always adored them, the happiness they bring, to me, to others. I'm convinced this preoccupation, this fixation, is intensifying, month by month.

I notice it when making tea, the inkling of clumsiness. The teabag falls from my fingers and misses the mug. I go to pick it up and I can't quite get my fingers and thumb to pinch the edge of it. I have to make three attempts.

Doesn't this happen to everyone from time to time?

'Stop fussing!'

'Sorry?'

I've said it aloud. I didn't mean to. It just popped out. I'm in the back of the shop, what we call the 'tea station'. Annie won't have heard my exact words.

'Nothing!' I call out.

I take Annie her tea and affect self-mockery.

'I'm such an idiot. I spilt hot water all over the table in there.'

I plan to place her mug close to the yellow roses. My hand is trembling, but I manage to put it down without upset.

'It's so annoying when you do that, isn't it?'

'I know.'

The incident is over. Annie has probably already forgotten it. I am persecuting myself by worrying about it, allowing myself to fear that she might see my mistakes.

I should make myself busy. We'll need a range of bouquets for the next few weeks, leading up to Christmas. They are pretty well our best period of the year, except possibly Valentine's Day.

There is a second workbench in a corner of the shop by the window display. I carry my mug over to it. We keep our flowers in small buckets, some on the floor, some on shelves. Their scent intoxicates me as I make a start with some antique carnations, some oriental lilies and four avalanche roses. I place them together in a vase. The carnations are a dusty pink and punch through the pallor of the cream roses and white lilies. I stand back. The bouquet needs another strong colour to offset the lighter flowers. I add sprigs of green bell, half a dozen of them, inserted around the edges and next to the wide open corolla of the lily that occupies the centre and focal point of the bouquet.

It's beautiful. The colours are gentle, subtle yet impressive. The shoots of green bell seem to spring out of the bouquet, as if growing within it, a touch of wildness thrusting through order.

I stand back again. I like it. It satisfies me.

The finishing touch is to bind the stems with twine and wrap the whole bunch in cellophane so that they hold their shape. I unreel green twine from the spool, lift the bouquet from the vase, and wind it around the stems. Then I cover the ugly twine with a strip of cream ribbon. I am almost there.

I pick up the flowers and they snag on the rim of the vase. The vase falls off the table and smashes into dozens of fragments. I try to hold on to the flowers, but I'm shocked and I can't and they slip out of my hands and slap on to the floor, where they bend and shed petals and fall apart.

Words are streaming through my head, a song, McCartney. I am, at one and the same time, singing and screaming.

11

GARY

February 2011

Years ago, long before her problems, I took her to France for a Valentine's Day surprise. From experience, I knew that there was generally no chance of prising her away from the shop on one of the busiest days of the year. If I'd even voiced the thought, it would have provoked uproar. Fortunately, this time, the day itself fell on a Sunday and the shop was closed except for organising deliveries. So I planned everything around a morning departure, and warned Annie that Kim wouldn't be coming in. Annie was happy enough, and she persuaded the Saturday girl, a sixteen-year-old who was genial and hardworking, to mind the shop while Annie scooted about town in the shop's van, dropping off bouquets.

'We're doing what!' Kim spluttered.

She was brushing her teeth and I'd told her we needed to get a move on.

'Ten o'clock ferry. I thought you'd be pleased.'

'What about the shop?'

'All taken care of. Annie's handling it.'

'Alone?'

'Of course not. Your girl'll be there. What's her name? Cathy.'

She nodded and resumed brushing. The burr of her electric toothbrush drowned out further discussion. She was, truth to tell, delighted to have the time off work, particularly a surprise, a couple of days across the Channel. But with Kim there had always to be a moment of guilt, of self-denial, as if a break away, which we took perhaps three times a year, was an indulgence incompatible with managing a serious business.

'It'll probably still be standing when you get back,' I said, 'and with a bit of luck, there'll be customers.'

She laughed, but she was annoyed. Part of her didn't like my flippancy. She'd built the business from scratch and demanded respect for that, which I had naturally, but I permitted myself the occasional facetious dig.

'It's Valentine's Day!'

I squeezed her from behind and her toothpaste dribbled from her chin on to my sleeve.

'I love you,' I said.

She scowled at me in the mirror.

We arrived in Calais just after midday. We were amongst the first to drive off the ramp and were quickly on the road south to Boulogne and Le Touquet.

There is a freedom about the roads of the Pas de Calais that is unlike anywhere I know. I suspect that it lies in the contrast between the congestion of south-east England, the tense motorway journey to the ferry, and the wide, Roman-straight autoroutes that roll across the empty hills and fields of northern France. We love it there, always have. The horizons are distant, the skies big and vaulting. That February morning, there was scarcely a vehicle on the roads. It seemed like we surfed along.

'When did we first start doing this?'

Her hand touched mine, lightly, as I changed gear to climb

the next long gradient.

'Pas de Calais, you mean? A few years.'

'Seven?'

'Seven! The lucky number, lucky for us anyway.'

She'd withdrawn her hand to let me drive. I grabbed it back and held on to it. Her skin was cold, and her hand felt small in mine, but I sensed its energy, a quick dextrous hand, used to picking up, splitting apart, cupping, pressing, binding, lifting and splaying, a hand accustomed to activity and precision. I pressed her fingers to my lips.

I'd booked our favourite fish restaurant in Le Touquet for lunch. Seven years ago, on Valentine's Day, I'd proposed to Kim there and she'd said no. I'd bought a ring, and I felt a fool. I'd convinced myself that we were both ready and of the same mind that marriage was right for us. I remember the embarrassment of her rejection, in the middle of the restaurant. It seemed to me that the room fell silent and I heard the ring box snap shut as I took it back and slipped it into my jacket.

Forty-eight hours later, we returned to Restaurant Perard, this time for dinner. By candlelight, we ate oysters and grilled turbot.

'Ask me again,' she said.

So I did, and she accepted. I hoped the same people were having dinner who had witnessed my botched attempt at lunch. We celebrated with champagne and baba au rhum.

The outskirts of Le Touquet flaunt wealth, exotic villas, all the colours of an artist's palette, owned by moneyed Parisians who drive up for weekends and most of July and August. The villas sit on long, wide avenues, designed to give the visitor a sense that they are approaching somewhere magnificent. The

Twenties and Thirties were the town's heyday, a time when Edward and Mrs Simpson fled there to escape the flash bulbs of London and Noel Coward held court at the Westminster Hotel. It can still attract a crowd, up to a quarter of a million in high summer. That's why Kim and I have always visited in the winter.

It was polar cold when we stepped out of the car. I'd failed to find a parking space in the town centre and had to resort to one of the paying car parks on the seafront. Kim wrapped her rug of a scarf around her, muffling her face against the bitter wind.

'Every time I see you in that thing I'm reminded how good it would be for a picnic.'

She laughed and pulled the red scarf tighter.

'And every summer you forget you ever had the thought.'

'Precisely.'

She clutched my arm and we headed into town.

'You should put it in your diary,' she said.

'If I kept one.'

We were comfortable that lunchtime, attuned to each other's needs and differences, safe in the knowledge that we planned to remain together, to see out the days left to us. We strolled along the street that led from the promenade to the restaurant and, without saying a word, I knew we were sharing the same thought: that this was the place where, in a formal sense, we started. We were re-tracing our history, as we did on every occasion we came back. It never failed to re-awaken the memory, to irradiate that moment in Restaurant Perard when I'd asked and she'd said yes.

They had kept our usual table for us, as I knew they would, a table for two in the window, overlooking, of all places, a florist's shop and a funeral director. This was the table where the decision had been taken. We'd lunched or dined at it half a dozen times since, every year, invariably in the deep of winter.

We ordered two glasses of Vouvray and a velouté of langoustine with a cognac cream, followed by lobster.

'What shall we do with the rest of the day?' I asked.

'Bike ride?'

'Will we be up to it?'

'I will.'

It was true. Whatever she'd eaten, it would never deter her from exercise, if she'd set her mind to it. Food was, if anything, a fuel, a spur to action. She once complained when I said I couldn't face making love after a particularly immoderate dinner. She put it bluntly. I must have known the plan was to make love, so why had I not taken that into consideration when choosing my meal? I was taken aback by how angry she was.

'We could postpone until tomorrow night,' I suggested.

'I might not feel like it then.'

This was early on. I had yet to grasp how capricious she could be, her spectrum of spontaneity, her exhibited need not only to enjoy the moment, but to exploit it to the full. Delay is death, she'd say.

When they brought the lobster, it looked polished. Its orange-brown shell gleamed, streaked with light. It sat on a bed of green leaves, with two halved lemons carefully wedged within the embrace of its hefty claws. The lobster's eyes had the lustre of buffed jet. They gazed at us reproachfully.

Each mouthful had the freshness of the sea, this morning's catch. The saltiness spiked my tongue, then the flesh softened into a malty mush. I drank some of the Vouvray.

'Near perfection,' I commented.

'Your standards are too high!'

She cracked open a claw and forked lobster meat out of the shell.

'There won't be better,' she added.

We hired bicycles on the waterfront and set off down the long, ruler-straight promenade. The cold bit into my hands, but there were short intervals of sunshine when the grey sea shimmered. Out on the horizon a line of dark tankers was heading west through the Channel.

We slowed to allow a number of lycra-clad joggers to pass.

'I've been thinking,' Kim said, as they swept by. 'We ought to talk about having a baby.'

'Now?'

She knew that I wasn't enthusiastic. I hadn't said no, but I was never the one to bring up the subject. I suspected she'd decided the bike ride would give her an opportunity to discuss it without having to face me. I could have put it off, but that was what I'd been doing for the better part of a year and since Kim was plainly not going to drop it, I reluctantly gave in.

We rode past a line of beach huts, decked out in a harlequin of bright, summer colours: blue, yellow, pink and lime green. An elderly man sat in his doorway on a canvas chair, smoking a stubby pipe. He looked as if he belonged to a different season, perhaps a different century. He waved his pipe as we flew by.

The conversation we were about to have had the potential to spoil the day. I tried to keep it light.

'What did you want to say, my love?'

'It's more to do with what you have to say, Gary.'

She pushed on ahead of me as the cycle lane narrowed to a

single track and we met an oncoming party of children carrying tennis racquets.

'You know what I think,' she called back. 'I want to try.'

Like so much of Le Touquet, the promenade dates back to the nineteen-twenties. No two villas are the same. They are loosely *art deco* in design, but with hints of Alsace, even the Netherlands. The shapes of roofs and gables are unlike any you'll find elsewhere in northern France. They're playful, idiosyncratic, designed to amuse, what they like to call 'holiday architecture'. It's as if the town has made a municipal decision to announce to the world: *When you enter Le Touquet, you leave the quotidian behind. Here is fantasy! Here is excess!*

What was I to say? Kim, too, knew my position.

'It's not that I'm totally opposed. I worry about you and how you'll cope with the birth and then looking after the baby.'

'Why on earth do you worry? I'm strong. I'm stronger than you. I'll be fine.'

I was skirting around the issue of her impatience.

'Do you think you'll want to make the time for a baby?'

'What do you mean? Of course! Why not?'

'Sometimes I feel you get a little grumpy if things don't go well. You know, if they don't go to plan.'

Kim suddenly braked and stopped. She dismounted and turned to me.

'What exactly are you getting at, Gary? If I hear you right, you're suggesting I won't have the staying power, the kindness, to care for my own baby properly. What's the word you always like to use on these occasions? You think I lack *composure*.'

I was desperate to find a way back, to avoid wrecking the day.

'You want this baby very much?' I said.

'Don't you! Don't dodge the question. That's what you think, isn't it? You look at me and you say to yourself "This bad-tempered bitch shouldn't have a child!" Isn't that it?'

'No, that's way more than I think. It's nothing like that.'

'Then what *is* the problem?'

'Perhaps there isn't one.'

'Make up your mind, for God's sake!'

She stepped off her bike and started to wheel it back down the promenade. I sensed all the energy and joy of the day drain away. We walked together, not speaking, trapped in the sullen aftermath of argument. It felt colder again. *L'homme à la pipe* had vanished from his doorway. People were quitting the beach.

'What would you want to call him or her?'

She pulled up.

'Are you serious? We have a row about one of the most important decisions a couple ever has to make, and then you carry on as if nothing has happened.'

'I'm trying to make amends.'

'Unbelievable!'

She walked on, pushing her bike ahead of her. Then she remounted the saddle and pedalled on until she was out of earshot. I took my time and followed her. As I drew level, she freewheeled for a while.

She smiled and reached across to take my hand.

'If it's a girl, she will be Adrianna.'

12

KIM

26th January 2017

Blackbird singing in the dead of night....... I don't know why the song is playing in my head, but I can't silence it. The same lines, always the first verse. McCartney's voice, of course, singing to me over and over. I can feel his lyrics shaping my mouth. *Only waiting for this moment to arise.*

Perhaps I'm trying to comfort myself before the scan. The song started as I entered a miniscule room where you're asked to undress and leave all your clothes and valuables in a locker. Apparently, the scanner will wipe clean your credit cards and stop your watch for good.

I'm nervous, no point in pretending I'm not. They have done their best to reassure me, but it's the noise everyone talks about that terrifies me and the length of time the examination could take. Some people can be in there for two hours.

'It won't be that long, Kim,' the operator tells me. Her name, she says, is Liz. 'We'll be done in under the hour, and we'll give you earplugs and headphones. The noise isn't too bad.'

She escorts me into the MRI lab and invites me to lie on the narrow table that faces the scanning cylinder. I stretch out, feet to the scanner, my head resting on a large pillow. Liz holds my hand as she explains.

'We're investigating your lower back today. The scanner's

going to give us really detailed images that can tell us if there's much damage down there.'

Much? I've only fallen a couple of times, I think. Perhaps more than a couple, but I'm not in pain. When Dr Bruce said that he wanted to have an MRI done, it struck me he was making a colossal fuss about nothing. I wouldn't have bothered, but Gary pleaded with me and I gave in. I can't bear the way he frets over me. It's not his body, for God's sake, not his state of health.

'The coil just sits over your waist like this.'

Liz places a large plastic hoop around me. It may not be plastic, but it looks like it. I can't tell.

This is how they propose to scan my spine and lumber. So far, the noise is tolerable, like several marching bands far off in the distance. I might be on a sixth-floor balcony, above the streets of Belfast on 12th July, at the height of the marching season.

I like the lighting. The room is filled with a soft indigo and inside the cylinder there is a low violet light, designed to soothe patients like me, I guess.

Liz raises my legs and wedges a cushion under my knees. She hands me a set of white headphones and mimes that I should put them on.

Peter Bruce is clearly worried about me. He tries to conceal his anxiety, but I can tell, and when he discovered that there would be a five month wait for a scan on the NHS, he asked me if we would consider going privately. Gary answered before I could get a word in. So, that's another grand out of our bank account.

Apparently, I'll have a follow-up consultation with a

radiologist, when I can discuss the results. So far, I have resisted asking too many questions, and I probably haven't been entirely honest with Peter Bruce about my symptoms. If I feel well enough in myself, I don't want to canvass a range of diagnoses that could ruin my life. I'll put up with this scan, but I don't doubt that when I'm called back, I'll get the all-clear.

Liz has passed me what she calls 'the emergency bulb'. Evidently, if I panic or feel uncomfortable, I can squeeze this rubber ball and it will immediately set off an alarm and stop the scanner. I'm even more nervous now. What kind of emergency might happen? Do most people panic?

The table jolts and starts to rise. Once it is level with the cylinder, it comes to rest, again with a jolt. Liz explains that, in the next few minutes, the table will travel into the cylinder and she will then leave the room to operate the scanner from a separate control box. So, I'm in the studio. She's in the director's gallery. I wonder why she can't run the machine standing next to me. I imagine there are potentially lethal rays that might escape the cylinder and poison her.

All this fuss!

The table moves forward very slowly. The tranquil violet light is appealing, but the curve of the upper wall of the cylinder is directly above my face, mere inches between us. I immediately begin to sense panic. It's hard to quell the claustrophobia, or perhaps it's the fear of claustrophobia and how that might feel, a fear so close to the thing itself that one easily leads to the other.

They think it's my spine, that there's damage to at least one of the vertebrae. Who knows? I fell in the woods. I slipped on our terrace at home and ended up hitting my knees hard on the paving stones. Another time, I fell first thing in the morning, getting up from our bed. For a few seconds, I lost all feeling in my legs and as soon as I attempted to stand, I crumpled.

I think Gary would have gone along with my belief that these were all unrelated accidents were it not for what happened on New Year's Eve.

The scanner is in full swing now. God knows what Liz is asking it to do, but the noise is demented and changes dramatically every few minutes. A surging piston is suddenly followed by a heavy, pulsing alarm – as if prisoners had escaped – or I'd escaped – and then a long, high groan takes over. My friend, Penny, warned me it would be like this. She was scared stiff when she went through it. I think I'm managing better than that. Penny said she was shaking like a wet dog when they finally released her.

Liz's voice is gentle, just like a nurse's, in my headphones.

'We're starting the second test, Kim. All going well so far.'

The second of what? How many tests are there? Three? Fifteen?

We'd been invited to a party on New Year's Eve, at the Dobbs', Chloe and Patrick. They were neighbours of ours, but we didn't know them at all well. They hadn't been to our house, and we generally just chatted for a few minutes in the street. But, for whatever reason, they'd decided that the close of the year was the time to get to know us better.

I wore the navy dress Gary had presented me with on Christmas Day, and black heels. We'd had a good Christmas, only the two of us, but fun. I gave Gary a waterproof jacket, one he could wear on long hikes in the Highlands.

I'd been feeling fine during the day. We'd shared a bottle of wine over lunch, not something we usually do, but it was the festive season after all. I took a rest in the afternoon, dozing in front of the television. We dressed about seven, resisted the temptation to brace ourselves with another glass before the party, and turned up at the Dobbs' place a little after eight.

I remember Chloe opening the door and, as we were taking off our coats, she just blurted out:

'Where did you get that dress? It's lovely, Kim!'

'Thank you, Chloe. You look great too.'

'Not like you, though. You look fabulous!'

So, the party started well. I joined a group of their friends in the sitting room, feeling confident and, unusually, attractive. There were a number of faces I recognized, but Sally was the only other guest I knew as a friend. We'd joined the same cycling club a number of years ago and met up occasionally on weekend runs.

'How are you?' she asked me. There was a hint of concern about her that surprised me.

'Fine,' I said. 'In fact, having had the praise of our hostess ladled over me, more than fine.'

'Haven't seen you out with the club recently.'

'No,' I said, 'I tend to bike on my own these days, or sometimes with Gary. But I'm planning to go on Saturday's run. I'll see you there.'

She took up a wine bottle she found on the table next to where she was standing and poured me a glass. She'd obviously had a few. Gary decided he would leave us to it.

'Handsome husband you've got there, Kim. Cheers!' She grazed her glass against mine. 'Here's to a bloody good year for us all!'

I sipped my wine slowly. We had a long night ahead of us. No one was expected to leave until we'd brought in the new year, so I planned to pace myself.

I glanced around while Sally ploughed her usual furrow. She's a bit older than I am, fifty or so. Cycling is really all we have in common. She's on her own, used to her own company, and given half a chance, she won't hesitate to tell you how horrified she is by the government's lack of support for sport, in despair about the NHS's failure to promote healthy living. I usually try to ignore her rants.

It was a striking room, large enough to support two chandeliers and floor-length cream curtains. Two leather sofas had been pushed to the walls to make room for the party guests to stand around and chat, and perhaps later dance.

I suppose we had been talking for ten minutes or so when my glass suddenly fell out of my hand. I watched it while it bounced on the pale green carpet and threw red wine over it. I couldn't believe I'd done it. I was mortified and, oddly, unable to move.

Chloe raced over.

'Don't worry! I'll clear it up in a jiffy. Pour yourself another glass.'

Sally had already done so and handed it to me. I took a large swig and hovered over Chloe as she dabbed the spilt wine and soaked it up in handfuls of kitchen towel.

'Attention seeker!'

Gary was at my elbow, trying to make me laugh about it.

'I feel such an idiot,' I said.

'Come on. It could happen to anyone.'

'I just lost my grip.'

'As I say, happens to all of us, my love, at some time or other.'

He was always supportive, Gary, always keen to offer the kinder interpretation, the salve that enabled me to recover and move on. It was the same if I had a crisis at work. If I was having problems with a customer, Gary would invariably come up with a form of words, the percipient phrase that would resolve our differences. He'd been a mediator, when common sense was called for, all my married life.

He could see that Chloe was struggling to remove the dark wine stain. When she looked up, I couldn't meet her eye. I knew I'd spoilt her evening. She was going to greet the new year with a ruined carpet. Gary decided to find a solution in the kitchen. He came back with a soggy J-cloth. He urged Chloe out of the way and set about soaking and scouring the stain. I could tell he was determined he would remove it. He wasn't going to give up until it was clear to him that he'd got the colour out and that the carpet would recover. I don't think it bothered him that he was in the middle of a party and that the other guests found his zeal strange.

To hell with them! He was doing it for me. For a moment, I wanted to sing.

'How's the business?' Sally asked.

'Good. Terrific over Christmas and should be through to Valentine's Day. It's been crazy, frankly. How's yours?'

Sally had clearly asked how my business was going in order to tell me about hers. She placed her glass carefully on the mantelpiece and looked around the room, as if she was about to divulge a state secret.

'I've got a bit of a dilemma.'

'Yes?'

'I've been offered a new post. With a charity.'

'Congratulations! What you've always wanted. What's the charity do?'

'It's a hospice. You know, looks after the dying in their final stages. Palliative care. But it wasn't the charity I wanted to discuss. It's a question of loyalty.'

'To your present employers?'

'Yes.'

'Haven't you been there for years?'

'Fifteen.'

'Exactly.'

'That's what gives me the dilemma.'

'They can't object if you want to leave.'

'Loyalty matters.'

I burst out laughing. I didn't mean to, but the impulse was overwhelming. Loyalty matters! I felt a surge of wild delight at the absurdity of it. I embarrassed Sally. She hated it that everyone was staring at us, disapproving of my lack of inhibition. I couldn't care less and stared back at them, but Sally had had enough of me for one party, and she sidled away to join a couple at the other end of the room.

Left on my own, I quietened down. Standing next to Sally, in all her discomfort, I'd felt confident, aggressively so, sure that there was no shame attached to my *boutade*, my volcanic glee. But now I was oddly still, rooted to the spot.

The rest is vague. Several people have told me what they think occurred, including Gary, but nothing they've said seems familiar. I simply can't remember any more than that, without warning, I fell. That's too dramatic. I crumpled. My knees gave way and I collapsed. My wings were broken and I descended from the sky. I didn't lose consciousness, but at the same time I couldn't grasp what was happening. Gary stood over me. I looked up into his worried face. Arms supported me, lifted me, held me while I regained my feet. It was all over, I would guess, in less than a minute.

They all concluded it was drink, of course. Chloe, Patrick, the rest of them: they put two and two together, the spilt wine, the loud laughter and finally losing my balance, and it all added up to me being pissed, too pissed to handle myself properly.

But it wasn't.

A series of fast pulses thuds through the MRI cylinder, then the repeated groans of another alarm. I am tired, worn out by the violence of endless noise and disciplining myself not to panic or surrender to the fear that streams through my body.

I close my eyes.

Eventually, it stops. Silence. It's like lying in a bed at a friend's isolated cottage deep in the countryside, surrounded by woodland, in the dead of night. There is not a sound, not a twig cracked or grass blown.

Then the table moves slowly backwards and I am drawn out of the cylinder. I exchange violet light for indigo, and Liz is waiting for me. She relieves me of my headphones and lifts away the coil from my waist.

'There. That wasn't too bad, was it?'

She gives me her hand as I swing my legs round and step off the table.

'We'll have the results in about a week or so,' she says.

Waste of time is what I'm thinking.

13

GARY

October 2018

I've decided that I should get a car. Everyday shopping is easily done on foot, but I've plans to re-decorate and perhaps buy one or two items of furniture. I'll need a vehicle to transport them.

Fraser's is a two-pump garage at the far end of the village. He makes his money from supplying fuel and servicing islanders' cars and vans and tractors, but he usually has three or four used vehicles for sale on his forecourt.

I took a walk down there, in between showers, and found Fraser wiping oil from his hands with a tartan rag. I cast my eye over the two vehicles he had on show, a Ford Focus and a Toyota 4X4.

'I was wondering when you'd drop by,' Fraser said.

He threw the rag onto a workbench and came towards me, hand extended.

'Was it inevitable I would?'

'No, not inevitable, but I'd say likely.'

He'd convinced himself that he had a sale and began to open the driver's door of the Ford. I noticed it had leather seats.

'I have known people who've come to the island and managed without, but they're either fanatical about running and hiking, or short-stayers.' He tapped the glass behind the steering wheel.

'Twenty-eight thousand. Low mileage, wouldn't you say?

'Just the two you have?' I asked.

'For the moment.'

'What about the Toyota? How much has that done?'

Fraser appeared surprised. He'd got me pegged for a small saloon. What did I want with a heavy 4X4 with a flat bed on the back? I thought I should explain.

'It's for transporting things. I might want to get some new furniture. That sort of thing.'

Fraser opened the tailgate of the Hilux and laid it flat.

'Big beast, this one. Two and a half litre diesel. More than you need?'

'Not sure. What's the mileage?'

Fraser had anticipated the question and already poked his head inside the cab.

'Ninety-two,' he said. 'It's hefty, but these engines go on for ever. She'll do twice that, easy, and you don't get one at this price without the mileage.'

I moved to the front of the vehicle to remind myself of the figure on the card propped up on the dashboard.

'I'll give you six thousand.' This was the difficult moment. 'In cash.'

'Cash?'

Fraser was a wily old bird. He'd traded vehicles for years, and he knew how to assess his customers. But I had no choice. I'd drawn out nearly all the money I had in my bank account shortly before leaving England. I'd left a small amount in credit, just under two hundred pounds, simply to avoid awkward questions about why I was closing the account. I knew there was no prospect of opening a new one in my assumed name and the same went for credit cards. I managed to persuade Angus to give me an account at his stores, but for any other purchase cash was my only option.

'You drive a hard bargain, Mr Montrose,' Fraser said.

'You'll take it?'

'It will do, yes.'

Fraser threw in a tank of diesel and dropped the keys into my hand. The Hilux started first time and I drove off the forecourt and took the road north.

It had been an unnecessary precaution, but I'd taken out the money over a period of several days and from a number of different branches and ATMs. With each new withdrawal, I'd expected to be challenged, for the ATM to announce that I had reached the maximum allowed in one month or for the bank teller to query this sudden change of behaviour. I waited impatiently in queues. If I caught anyone's eye, I suspected he or she knew something, had seen me the day before with hundreds in cash.

But then I realised that all my anxiety was groundless. The truth was that no one cared a damn. As far as my bank was concerned, as long as I didn't exceed the limit of my overdraft, and I didn't, I was free to take out money as frequently as I wanted it and spend it how I liked. By the end, I had over twenty thousand pounds in notes, neatly stacked in a black attaché case, as if I were about to pay off kidnappers or buy a consignment of cocaine.

In its northern parts, the island is barren. The road deteriorates into a rutted track, so seldom used these days that it's gradually returning to the surrounding scrub. The Hilux had no trouble with the rough ground, though, or the potholes, and I reached the north coast without difficulty.

A storm was gathering strength out at sea. Dark, towering thunderheads heaped up on the horizon. They would make their way inland in the course of the next hour, but for now there was a cold wind and damp in the air. I stepped out of the truck and stood on the cliff, marking how the grey clouds rushed together and swept apart far out at the world's edge.

What's left for me, Kim? I've come to this island with a stash of money and no idea what to do with the rest of my life. People are friendly enough, but I've no friends as such here, no one I can talk to frankly, confide in. Most nights I sit alone in my cottage and drink whisky. It requires a deal of self-discipline not to do it during the day as well. What should I do, my love? I know I lost much of you a long time ago, but now that you've gone completely, I have no purpose, at least none beyond evasion and survival.

You were always the cheerful one! You saw the absurdity in disasters, the humour in reversals. Even when you were impatient, you could snap out of a mood while I sank into it, sullen. I watched you hover above while I drowned in my own melancholy. You were right to shout at me, to demand better.

And now?

Out of habit, I took my phone out to check for texts or emails. There were, of course, none. I'm not sure why I picked up this pay-as-you-go device. I guess that I'm so habituated to having a mobile I can't imagine life without one. But I haven't given out the number and I've abandoned my email account. No one can reach me, unless it's by random selection, a media survey, a cold call about a road accident I haven't had.

My hands were frozen. I pocketed the phone and looked out

to sea. I could smell the rain advancing, like a massed army. It wouldn't be long now.

Rescue me, my darling!

Although I could hear the timbre of her voice, its cadences, there were no words in reply, no comforting thought. I knew she was listening out there, weighing up what to say, but unable to speak, just like the closing months, the last few furlongs of waiting.

Did I come here to make a new life? I suspect that part of me saw it as a stay of execution, a deferment of the inevitable, whilst another part was buoyed up by the hope that I might escape, might run to the end of the earth scot-free and unpunished.

You will forgive me, Kim, won't you?

You always have.

You have to.

The rain came in hard. It took me by surprise, even though I'd watched the storm creep steadily towards me. The sky was coal black and I knew the rain would last a good two hours. It struck my face and hands, spikey jabs on my skin, skidding off my chin and thickening my fingers, the sound of firecracker bursts as it pelted my jacket. I could scarcely keep my eyes open.

I ran for the Hilux. Inside, the rain hammered the windscreen. It quickly steamed up and I lost sight of the cliff and the tumultuous sea beyond.

You thought you'd got away with it, didn't you? When we caught the train into London to get the results of your MRI, you were sure they'd find nothing wrong.

'Don't worry,' you said. 'It'll be fine.'

We stood in front of a woman in a creased white coat. A stethoscope embraced her neck and pens piled in her breast pocket. I tried to read her expression, but she was an expert, giving nothing away. She smiled and ushered us to chairs at her desk.

'You'll be pleased to hear the results are good,' she said.

I silently thanked her for her directness, for saving us the wretchedness of anticipation.

'We found no evidence of damage, Kim, or disease. A clean bill of health, you might say.'

Kim threw me a glance, *I told you so* blazing in her wide eyes.

I was delighted, of course, and relieved. The last thing I would have wanted was for the scan to have discovered any injury or malignancy. At the same time, I did want to know what was wrong with Kim, what had caused her to fall, and I had hoped the MRI would provide an answer.

Kim was beginning to get up from her chair.

'Just a sec,' I said. 'Is that all there is to it? We expected we'd find out more about why Kim's been falling over.'

'It's obviously nothing to worry about, darling,' Kim said. 'We can go.'

I put my hand out to detain her, gently touching her arm.

'Hang on. Sit down, please.'

I turned to the consultant.

'Shouldn't you be running other tests? I mean, aren't there other scans or investigations you could do? She's collapsed half a dozen times in less than two months. That can't be right, can it?'

The consultant had met people like me before. She leaned forward, removed her glasses, placed them methodically on her desk, steepled her hands. I thought she might be about to pray.

'I understand, but you see when you asked for an MRI, that was the only test you were buying. Dr Bruce wrote to me about Kim's symptoms and there was a chance – only a chance, mind – that they may have been the result of harm to the vertebral column. We now know that area is healthy and undamaged, and we can move on. If Kim is concerned and feels that she would like further tests to be done, she can visit Dr Bruce and I'm sure he will contact the hospital to arrange them.'

'It takes weeks for appointments to come through on the NHS,' I said.

'I'm afraid that's how it works. We are very stretched.'

Kim had had enough. She was on her feet and impatient.

'Gary, it's not this doctor's responsibility. Come on. We should go and let her get on with her work.'

She grabbed my arm, tugged me out of the chair. I was reluctant to leave. I knew that there was nothing more we could achieve by staying, but this consultant was the only senior doctor we had to talk to. I thought she ought to be able to give us better advice.

'We are a bit anxious, I'm afraid.'

'I can see that,' she said.

'No, we're not! Let's go!'

Kim clutched at my sleeve again and I gave in. We thanked the consultant and left her room.

There were four flights of stairs to descend to reach the street. I took my time, sorry to leave the building where the answer to Kim's problem could, I was certain, be found. It was as if we were stepping away from a vital source of help, from a cure, if that was what was needed.

If it wasn't a spinal injury or disease, what could it be? What caused someone to experience a series of sudden and unexplained falls, a middle-aged woman who had been extremely fit, who had no previous record of illness or disability, and who appeared to be alert and strong at other times? That seemed to rule out, say, dementia. What else did that leave? A brain tumour?

'What do we do next?' I asked.

'We stop worrying. That's what.'

She sounded convinced, but I noticed that she held on firmly to the banister as we went down. It frightened me to see her like that. She had always been, how shall I put it, a bright-and-breezy kind of person, dismissive of palaver. There were never storms in her teacup. She got on with life, confident in her resilience, her health. Now, as she took each stair, there was a momentary hesitation. She looked almost fragile.

'You're not right, you know. There's something wrong with you, Kim.'

She stopped and smiled up at me.

'Nonsense, my love. I'm fine.'

The rain raked my windscreen and pooled at the bottom of the glass. It caught what grey light there was left in the day and bent it into beautiful, coloured specks. I thought about how loud the hammering was, the drumming on the roof, a deep sound, an ancient sound, unlike the brittle, metallic stippling I could hear behind me on the flat bed of the Hilux. This was local rain, the kind of merciless autumnal storm you could only experience on an island off the west coast of Scotland.

How wrong you were! That you thought you were inherently well and, later, that you could beat it, was a stark irony. I remember all the years of physical strength, striking out over

Highland moors, golden with gorse, swimming in freezing lochs and tumbling rivers. I've seen you step out of an icy burn, naked on a winter's afternoon, and think nothing of the cold, towelling your slender, heavenly body. I've seen you laugh at minus-five.

All that became the history of another, didn't it? A past of such athleticism, such hardiness, could not be easily reconciled with what you turned into, my love, at the end. It was as if yesterday, your time in Scotland, your past, your *seachad*, mocked you, jeered at your infirmity, your broken wings, at your egregious suffering, bent into ugly, dimmed fragments.

The rain eased a little, enough for the windscreen wipers to be effective. I could at least see now. I swung the Hilux round and headed off on the road south. By the time I reached the village, the rain had stopped. I passed Fraser's garage. He was nowhere to be seen. I made a mental note that I needed to let him have the cash for the car in the next couple of days.

I climbed the track to the cottage and when I was, I suppose, a quarter of a mile away, I realised there was a police car parked outside. I was too far off to see what they were up to. I decided to leave the Hilux and walk the rest on foot. I might be able to climb the hill above the house and get a view of them without them seeing me.

14

KIM

12th February 2017

We don't generally play music in the shop. I always like to have a mixed playlist on standby, in case we need cheering up on a dreary winter afternoon when the shop is empty, but for the most part, Annie and I prefer to chat. I think I made an exception this morning because I couldn't drive out the memory of the pistons and thuds and alarms that made the MRI scan such a purgatory. So, we had The Beatles – *Blackbird*, needless to say – two Miles Davis tracks, a nod to Gary's desert island, and for sheer joy I added Julie London singing *Fly Me To The Moon*. Annie then insisted that we must have some Spice Girls and Oasis. Her youth, she said.

I'd begun work on a bouquet for Valentine's Day. I'd started with lilac Hyacinths and Amnesia roses and I was planning to add touches of white and green. We had no customers, and I was glad that I could get on without pressure or interruption. For once, my hands seemed to be coordinated, strong even, and I could drink a cup of tea and not spill any of it.

God knows what music was playing when she entered the shop. I can't remember and, in any case, I switched it off as soon as I recognised her. It was Sally.

'Good Lord!' she said.

She had the surprised look of someone who had never visited

a florist. It was certainly the first time she'd come to my shop.

'How lovely to see you,' I said.

'It's all so.' She paused. 'Colourful.'

'That's the aim.'

It was well over a month since I'd last seen her, at the New Year's Eve party, and we'd not been in touch in the meantime. I wondered what on earth had prompted her to call in on me at work.

I introduced Annie.

'Can we interest you in anything? We've just had a delivery of some fabulous orchids.'

Doesn't miss a trick, Annie.

'Or these very colourful tiger lilies.'

'Great colours, I agree,' Sally said. 'Actually, I just wanted to find out how you were, Kim. After the party.'

Six weeks ago.

Annie realised she was unlikely to make a sale, so she drifted into the back of the shop and resumed her silent work emailing invoices. I had an odd sense of having been abandoned, left to deal with Sally as best I could. I suspected that Annie detected an impulsiveness about her.

'I was in the area. I thought, on the off chance you might be around, I'd pop in. I've been worried.'

'It's kind of you.'

'Did you hear from Chloe?'

'No, I think I blotted my copy-book there. You?'

'No. Not a dicky bird. That evening must have been a nightmare for you. Bloody awful, wasn't it?'

I didn't need reminding. For the last few weeks, it had been uncomfortable to walk down our street, aware that the gossip had spread and that our neighbours now viewed me as the drunk who had ruined Chloe's carpet. I had sparked a new interest in me. Whether they gave a moment's thought to the possibility that I might have been ill, I rather doubted.

'Did they run any tests?' Sally leaned forward on the workbench to emphasise her concern. 'I know it's none of my damned business, but friend to friend, you know.'

Her gravity struck me as ironical. She might have rung me on New Year's Day, or any of the following days, to ask me how I was, but instead she'd left it until now. I could have died in the interval. *Friend* I thought was pushing it. I didn't want to tell her about the subsequent falls, the scan. She impressed on me a curious sense of duty, as if I were accountable to her, obliged to explain my behaviour in clinical terms. I resisted.

'I appear to be fine.'

'A one-off?'

'Seems that way.'

Are people, let's call them acquaintances, owed the truth? Of course, I believe that truth is ordinarily preferable to lies. But in these circumstances? What purpose is served by letting her into my secrets, my clumsy episodes, the uncertainty that inevitably follows examination? Another story to entertain her colleagues over a drink after work? *Bavardage*. No more. Or would it alarm her? She might take to phoning me in the middle of the night, dropping round to the shop at busy times. I couldn't bear that. Better to mislead her, a slight deceit that allowed her to walk away contented and let me off her hook.

'Did you take the hospice job?' I asked.

'It's exhausting.'

'I'm sure. How long have you been there?'

I was desperate for a customer to burst into the shop and demand my attention.

'Three weeks. Longest three weeks of my life. It's not so much the physical strain - though that's bad enough. It's the bloody emotional stuff, Kim. They're all in such a terrible state when they reach us. They look appalling, frankly. We do allow some short respite stays, but mostly they have to be in shooting distance of dying to be admitted. Two or three weeks on the whole. Nightmare.'

'Will you stick at it?'

'Oh yes! Of course.' Sally sighed. 'I'm just in need of a bloody good holiday. That's all.'

'Anywhere in mind?'

'Not really. Anyway, I couldn't possibly take leave for at least another month.'

I thought back to the weekends we'd cycled together, to Sally's evident passion for the outdoors, for cycle tracks in the wilderness.

'Gary and I had a wonderful week in the Highlands a couple of years ago. The cycling was really good.'

'In March?'

'It's lovely all year round. I know it's easier to get to Rome or Madrid. Everyone says it. But you'd love it up there. Let me send you details. Leave me your email.'

I suspect Annie had realised that I was trying to bring the conversation to a close because she came over, a sense of urgency about her. She pressed my arm.

'You know those bouquets we said we'd have ready for lunchtime?'

'Oh God, yes! I'd forgotten. Sorry.'

'They'll be here in twenty minutes.'

Sally took her cue.

'No, of course. I mustn't keep you. You've got your work to do. Let me just give you this.'

She scribbled her address on a post-it and fixed it to the workbench.

'Look after yourself, Kim. Keep in touch.' She wheeled to the door and, as she slipped onto the street, she called out 'See you!'

I turned to Annie and said thank you.

15

GARY

October 2018

I succeeded in climbing the cliff above the cottage and from there could look down on the police car and what turned out to be a solitary policewoman, standing at my front door, evidently unsure whether to stay or go. She took a step back from the house and appeared to survey the windows, particularly upstairs, trying to confirm, I could only imagine, whether or not the place was empty.

It occurred to me that I could let her reach the conclusion that no one was in and drive away. On the other hand, if I did that, she would return at some time when I wasn't anticipating her and I might be caught off-guard. I decided to drop down the hill and confront her.

As I approached the cottage, she was in semi-profile. I guessed she couldn't be more than twenty-five. I was starting to hope that that was reassuring. If it had been a serious matter, they would have sent someone older and more senior.

She turned. Tall, glasses, attentive.

'Mr Montrose?'

'Aye, that's me.'

Aye? Nerves, of course.

'WPC Cullen, sir.'

I could have kicked myself. Every time I'd used the word

'aye' it had been clumsy or simply theatrical.

I unlocked the front door and led the way inside. She took off her police bowler hat, jammed it under the arm of her tunic and, fastidiously, cleared her glasses of loose strands of blonde hair. I steered her towards the kitchen and offered her tea as I took down mugs from the dresser.

'No, I won't, thanks. It's just a courtesy call, Mr Montrose. We like to make contact with everyone on the island at some point. I'm sorry it's taken rather longer in your case than we'd have liked.'

'That's quite alright.'

I wasn't entirely comfortable that she'd simply come to say hello. She was uneasy, lacking in confidence, as if she had something urgent or significant to say, but couldn't quite bring herself to voice it. I let the kettle boil while she assembled her thoughts.

'We are a law-abiding community,' she said. 'I'd like you to know that.'

'I've no reason to doubt it, officer.'

'Do call me Hannah. Everyone does round here.'

I dropped a teabag into my cup and splashed water onto it. Careless, as usual. Hot water bounced back out of the mug and dripped from the edge of the table. Hannah Cullen appeared to study it. I wondered if she disapproved.

'We have the occasional burglary,' she continued. 'Pilfering. Vandalism. Minor stuff. Kids mainly, as you might imagine.'

She raised her eyes from the spilt water and looked steadily at me.

'I thought you should know.'

'Thank you.'

'It's as well to keep things under lock and key, bolt your door at night. That sort of thing.'

'I will. It's very good of you to take the trouble to come round and give me the warning.'

'No bother, sir.'

Our meeting was beginning to feel protracted. She could have brought me a leaflet, communicated all the stock advice in writing.

'There was one other matter, Mr Montrose.'

As if I hadn't anticipated it.

'Fraser, at the garage—'

'The Hilux?'

'Yes. He sold you a Toyota Hilux this morning, I believe.'

'True. He did.'

That, surely, was no infringement. I was beginning to feel watched. Was this the kind of surveillance all blow-ins were subjected to? In the absence of CCTV, were new people observed by the old, daily sightings passed on by word of mouth? The idea seemed far-fetched.

'You paid in cash.'

'As a matter of fact, I haven't yet, but yes, that's my intention.'

'Is that because you don't have a bank account, Mr Montrose?'

She was expecting to write down details.

'Isn't this a bit intrusive, Hannah. Do you mean up here in Scotland?'

'Anywhere, sir.'

I drank some tea. It burnt.

'No, no, I don't.'

'Is there a particular reason for that?'

'I've not been terribly well treated in the past. By banks. I don't think I've been valued as a customer. And interest rates are so low, I'd rather deal in cash.'

'That's up to you, of course, but I don't have to tell you, sir, it is unusual.'

Had I said too much, been too defensive? Perhaps I wasn't obliged to justify my behaviour.

'I suppose it is. I hadn't really given it much thought.'

'No, no, well as I say, entirely your choice.'

'May I ask how you know that I paid for the car in cash?'

'Fraser usually informs us about new sales. We like to keep an eye on trade in vehicles. Check up on whether they have been taxed and insured.'

'Of course. Look, I'm sorry. I will be on to all that later today.'

'You're not an easy person to trace in police records, Mr Montrose.'

She placed what seemed to me surprising emphasis on my name, as if she didn't quite trust the way she'd pronounced it or thought that she'd perhaps been given the wrong spelling. She was waiting for me to respond.

'That's a good thing, surely? Do you need to trace me?'

'It's just routine. I couldn't find any car insurance either, or tax for a vehicle in your name.'

'Well, as I say, I'm planning—'

'On any previous vehicle.'

'I—'

She flipped closed her notebook and returned it to a pocket in her tunic.

'I won't keep you longer.'

I felt I'd escaped, narrowly.

'Do remember the security measures, won't you? I expect that you have quite a lot of cash here. The island's safe enough, but you are a bit remote, and there are some kids who'd see that as an opportunity, shall we say?'

She smiled, it seemed to me for the first time, and made her way to the door.

'Thank you for your time, Mr Montrose.'

She adjusted her bowler hat.

'Very good to meet you, sir, at last,' she said. I held the door open for her. 'I'm sure I'll see you soon.'

What this meeting has taught me is that I haven't been as careful or circumspect as I'd imagined. I thought I had been clever, covering my tracks, as they say, but it appears that no behaviour is beyond discovery, no concealment dark enough. My cash economy is suspect, my invisibility in national databases cryptic. To some extent, I shall have to live with that vulnerability. Trying to open a bank account would lead to further enquiries, which I can't risk.

But then, am I worrying unnecessarily? What do you think, my love? Should I even be making the effort to disappear? Isn't it impossible to cut oneself off these days? Entirely?

16

KIM

25th February 2017

I had such a vivid dream last night, and it involved my father, who's been dead for over a decade. I haven't dreamt about him, thought about him really, for years. After he left my mother, we had less and less to do with him. By the end, I was scarcely seeing him at all. I think, in the year he died, I saw him once.

But there he was, in the dream. I can't say what emotion, if any, I felt. Was I pleased to see him? It's hard to say. I don't know. He was just there and I accepted it.

Aged what? How old would he be? Forties, fifty perhaps. He died when he was fifty-nine. Heart attack, a massive one. In the dream, he's wearing a suit, in the circumstances a completely inappropriate navy suit threaded with narrow white stripes. He died in that suit, I believe.

We are on the edge of a field, in a car park, or it might be a recreation ground with a parking area. We appear to own a large van or, no, not a van, a 4X4 with two rows of seats in the cab. It's not an attractive vehicle, probably grey, but it's so dirty you'd struggle to say what the colour is. It's seen a lot of wear, outside and in, dents and scratches in the bodywork, hasn't been cleaned inside in living memory. For some reason, I know this vehicle belongs to my father, in his pinstripe.

My mother (in truth, dead too) is with us, and we're hanging around the 4X4, anxious to get away, but something makes it impossible for us to leave. I can't determine what it is, but it's powerful. We can't ignore it.

Suddenly, there's an explosion. I think I must have anticipated it because it happens just as I look round. I turn at the very moment of ignition, a loud thunderclap, when the sky cracks on the far side of the park, an eruption in red, orange, and yellow, threatening and noisy. Everywhere around us the car park is full of people we hadn't noticed before. They're panicking, floundering, shouting, while a pall of flint grey smoke falls over us.

My father wants to run in the direction of the explosion.

'I must help!' he yells above the crowd.

It's unclear what, if any, help is needed, what has exploded and what harm it has done, but my father is convinced that there must be victims and he wants to give assistance.

'We need you here,' my mother says.

'Nonsense!' my father replies. 'My services are required elsewhere.'

Services?

Then the scene leaps forward. He hasn't left us, and instead sits in the driving seat, incongruous in his smart suit in his shabby vehicle. He is trying to yank shut the driver's door, but I'm holding on to it, preventing him. This time, I'm the one yelling.

'Do you want me to drive?'

He doesn't reply and continues to drag at the door.

'Dad! Do you want me to drive?'

I'm hoarse from shouting and, presumably, the smoke.

The car park is at a standstill. Hundreds of cars are trying to leave the recreation ground. It's gridlock, paralysis.

I'm screaming.

'Let me drive, Dad!'

Reluctantly, I can tell, he lifts himself from the driver's seat, steps on to the tarmac, gives way.

'I don't know why you think you'll be any better at this than I am,' he comments.

I'm now reversing us out of our parking space, careful to avoid other vehicles that are manoeuvring behind us.

'How do you think you're going to get us out of here?' my mother asks, rather imperiously I sense, as if I owe it to her.

I have the 4X4 in a line of traffic waiting to exit the park. Most of us are prepared to queue, but the closer to the park gates I get, the more evident it is that cars are approaching from every direction. The darkness brought on by the smoke makes it increasingly probable that we'll hit each other.

I'm resigned to the likelihood that we will be here for some time.

My father and my mother are both soundly asleep.

17

GARY

October 2018

'Thanks, Angus.'

We had carried the ladder out of his store and placed it on the flat bed of the Hilux. I had to leave the tailgate down because of its length.

'You'll be wanting some rope, I imagine,' Angus said. 'As soon as you start climbing that hill of yours, it'll slide off the back and run all the way back to the village.'

'You can sell it twice over!'

'It wouldn't be the first time.'

He disappeared into the shop to fetch rope and I took a look around the Hilux to find useful fixing points.

It had come to me 'in drink', as they say. The idea, I mean. I had a glass of Islay malt waiting for me on the bathroom table. I was staring at myself in the small mirror above the basin, next to the Dali print. I had a swig of the whisky and pushed my face close to the reflection. I hadn't shaved for three days, black stubble in a fleshy field of purple and crimson. I could swear that, day by day, I was darkening. My face was bloodier, angrier, mottled like Red Verona Marble.

Is this what failure looks like, Kim?

Catastrophic thinking. My speciality. A predisposition to imagine the worst outcome of all those possible, a rapid nosedive into dejection and inconsolable grief. Stop making a fuss! That's what you'd have said, wouldn't you?

I needed a project, something to give each day a shape and a purpose. I had been filling the hours as best I could, vacuuming the cottage, cooking meals that involved hours of preparation, reading a newspaper from front to back or another chapter of Stark in Arabia. I'd lost all interest in music. I felt the lack of it, but the music I loved reminded me too keenly of her. So, I'd find myself trawling the internet for anything that sprang to mind and, if all else failed to crowd out thought, I'd go for a walk or pour myself another drink.

The moment had come to give all my time and energy to a task. I wanted to make something. My face changed as I had the thought. I was cheerful again, inspired.

The idea – call it a concept – was to create a memorial to Kim. I had yet to decide what form it might take. There were endless possibilities. She conjured up so many associations when I thought about her, so many images. It had to be substantial. It had to be visible at a distance, though perhaps not a great distance. I was imagining a landmark Struan Lamont might notice when he was out at sea. This would be an object taller than a man, smaller than a house.

The ladder was a start. I knew it was right as soon as the thought came to me. I wasn't sure whether it was a part or the whole, but it would certainly feature.

We tugged down on the rope and strapped the ladder to the Hilux. I thanked Angus for his help and stepped up into the driver's cab.

'You'll be careful not to clean your gutters in a high wind,' Angus said.

'I'll try not to.'

'Then I'll sleep easy in my bed. Away.'

I geared the Hilux and drove off the hard standing that acted as the stores' car park. The memorial being so inchoate, it hadn't seemed appropriate to tell Angus about my plans. If he thought I'd bought the ladder to deal with leaves and broken gutters, that was fine. The village would see my tribute to Kim in due course. Every instinct urged me to keep her death a secret, a private matter, but I knew that sooner or later I would have to admit it.

The cottage had an out-house that the owner must once have used as a workshop. An old carpenter's bench sat in a corner by the window. It had a wooden vice and one edge was a steel measure. The out-house had no heating, but there was a mains point, on which I could run one of the two-bar electric fires I kept in the cottage.

You'll like it, Kim. I'll do you proud, my love. I promise.

There had to be colour, vivid splashes of diverse colours. That much I already knew. The colours must be bright, closely juxtaposed, as flowers might be in a bouquet.

The ladder was three metres tall and made of hardwoods, Douglas Fir for the uprights, the 'stiles', and American Oak for the rungs, intended to endure, to survive harsh weather and not rot. I sat down at my desk and drew a sketch of it. It reminded me of rigging on a medieval ship. I studied the diagram and tried to imagine it painted. A rainbow pattern of colours was the easiest design to go for, but Kim would have found that too obvious. When she arranged flowers, she liked to surprise people with unlikely combinations and subtle variants on a single shade. I needed to come up with a unique sequence. I realised the solution would be to identify the colours I wanted to employ and attach a number to each. I could then work out how to paint the ladder as a mathematical series. It would be, above all, clever, like Kim herself.

I powered up my laptop and began to search the colour charts of paint manufacturers. I chose yellow first. There were foreseeable names that had the word 'daffodil' or 'lemon' or 'banana' in them, but then I discovered amusing shades like *Butter Biscuit* and *Lunar Falls*. Every primary colour subdivided into half a dozen variant hues. I realised I could paint the ladder in over forty different colours. I thought about how baffled Angus would be when I ordered that number of paint pots.

Raspberry Diva, *Enchanted Eden*, *Urban Obsession*, and all the rest, please, Angus.

'You're not setting up your own business, are you, Mr Montrose?'

The plan excites me. I swing open the door to the out-house, my workshop, and switch on the electric heater. Work starts today.

First, the ladder needs sanding down.

18

KIM

14th March 2017

I have just surrendered my watch, my three rings and an amber necklace. I am once again sitting in a waiting room, wearing a flowery cotton gown that is open at the back and, frankly, draughty and humiliating. I feel vulnerable and uncared-for. My own fault, of course. I came by myself because I didn't want Gary fretting around me during the examinations. They will be disagreeable enough without me having to calm his anxieties as well.

I fell again. I think that's what prompted me to agree to further tests. It was in the shop, fortunately not when I was dealing with customers. Annie was somewhere in the back. I felt my left foot simply go. There was no real forewarning, mere seconds to register a sense that my instep had crumpled. It had fallen over, and I went with it.

I was shocked. Strange how, as I looked around from my awkward seated position on the floor, nothing else had changed, how my beloved shop, built from scratch, was a silent and passive witness to my collapse. A moment before, I had been strong and competent and standing, and then I was sprawled on cold tiles, powerless and a little frightened.

They have taken blood, a number of phials. I am due to have a muscle biopsy later this afternoon. I gather that you feel as if your muscle is being gently tugged as it happens. For now, I sit in the anteroom to the EMG clinic. An electromyography, I was told, is a procedure that will assess the health of my muscles and the nerve cells controlling them. No one has explained to me what that's like, if I will experience pain. Still less has there been any discussion of what I might have, whether it's a disease, possibly a viral infection. Perhaps I just need to boost my vitamin intake, take more calcium or Omega 3.

I can't say that I have no concerns. I don't doubt I'll get over this, whatever 'it' is. After all, I've been fine almost immediately whenever I've fallen or dropped something. It can't, therefore, be serious. I suppose what worries me is that I've never before lost control of my body. I've never had to cope with my legs and hands and feet acting, as it were, independently of what I want them to do.

I'm producing excess saliva, I notice. That must be nerves.

Angela, who is to be my nurse this morning, takes my hand and, with an infinite gentleness I thank her for, guides me down a long corridor the colour of blue eggshells and through swing doors. Inside, the room is large, high-ceilinged and oddly comfortless.

'Come and sit over here, Kim.'

His voice is kind, reassuring, contrasts to the atmosphere of the room. He wears navy scrubs and what look like white plastic clogs.

'My name is Robert. Has anyone explained what we're about to do today?'

'Not really.'

Perhaps they have, but I can't remember any details.

Robert takes my hand, too, so Angela wasn't alone in doing

so. It must be usual practice, a technique of care. I am grateful, though at the same time it crosses my mind that if it's necessary to give such tangible comfort, what lies ahead may be worse than I'd anticipated.

'First of all, we'll give you a topical anaesthetic cream, which should reduce any soreness from the needles.'

What needles? Did they warn me about needles? I've forgotten.

'We'll be putting in a small number of needles – they're called electrodes – and we insert them into your muscles to test their responses. We can see how your muscles behave on this monitor, which is called an oscilloscope. Are you happy for us to go ahead?'

I nod. Who are *we*? Who are *us*? Angela stands by the door. She will play no part, I think, in the examination. There is no one else, other than Robert, in the room. It is a euphemism. *We* are the hospital, the medical profession, those qualified to find out what's wrong with me.

I feel slight numbness creeping through the muscles of my left arm, a peculiar loss of sensation, as if a part of me, so vital to my day-to-day existence, is separating from me, saying goodbye.

Robert bends down and pinches me just below my shoulder.

'Do you feel anything?' he asks.

'Yes,' I say, hesitant, unsure what I feel. 'But not as sensitive as usual.'

'Good. We'll proceed.'

He smiles at Angela, who I sense approaching me from behind. I was wrong. She has a rôle. She is going to stand next to me throughout, there to soothe and encourage.

They are aware of my fear. Their attentiveness suggests that. I won't call it fuss. It's not intrusive, but rather a quiet and solicitous tenderness. I would like to confess my phobic reaction to hypodermic needles, but I daren't. I don't want to appear squeamish, nor give them reason to discontinue the investigation.

There are all sorts of pain I can tolerate. I've sustained countless injuries hiking or cycling or swimming wild in mountain rivers. They don't bother me. Even childbirth I coped with, physically if not emotionally. But the very sight of a syringe and a hypodermic needle, let alone the short sharp needles they are lining up for me now, shudders me. The muscles in my stomach tighten and I feel a sudden coldness all over. I think it has to do with the thinness of the steel and the fragility of my skin as it is punctured. Is there perhaps some ancestral horror that colours this fear, Christ on the Cross?

I feel close to passing out. I look away from what Robert is doing, though I can't avoid being aware of it. He has finished with my arms. It is impossible to tell whether I have responded well or not. Did he have expectations? What does the oscilloscope say? Have my muscles performed?

He kneels down and repeats the procedure on my legs. He inserts a series of short needles into my left calf, one after the other. They sting like the devil. He indicates that I should raise my leg and tense the calf muscle and then lower the leg. Despite my fears, I can't help watching him. It's fascinating, even as they hurt and turn my stomach, to see the needles pierce me. I suppose it goes against every instinct to allow someone to penetrate your flesh. I feel the urge to vomit. I swallow hard to suppress it.

'Are you okay?' Angela asks. 'Do you need a break? We can stop for a few minutes, if you like.'

I want to answer, but my tongue feels too swollen to enable me to speak. Saliva dribbles on to my chin and Angela dabs me with a tissue. They assume my humiliated silence is consent and continue. Robert pushes another needle into my calf. He tells me to contract my muscles as hard as I can.

Gary should be here. I made a mistake in not asking him to accompany me. He wouldn't have been allowed into the EMG Room, but at least I would know that he was waiting for me outside, ready to take me in his arms and let me cry if I need to.

He has been so good about it all. He frets, which is annoying, but entirely because he cares. He tries to mask his apprehension, but he can't help himself, and I avoid discussion because I fear some of it might rub off on me. As soon as I'm free of these tests, I'm going to insist he takes me out for a meal. We'll go to The Chapter. Who cares about the expense? We'll order oysters and drink champagne.

How much longer?

Have I said it aloud? They have not responded, so I assume not. Robert looks up at me. There is sympathy in his eyes.

'Nearly there,' he says. 'Just the top of your right leg to go.'

He inserts an electrode into the thigh muscle. I know I should avoid looking at it, but I can't help catching a glimpse.

'My God, that hurts!'

'Sore?' he says. 'Sorry!'

It seems to me that this needle has gone further in than the others, possibly because the thigh muscle is so large by comparison.

'Can you bend your right leg and lift it, please Kim.'

I do as I am instructed. The oscilloscope sits on a table near my feet. As I raise my leg, a wave of action passes across the screen. I presume that is a good sign. My thigh muscle has responded to the stimulus.

Robert gives nothing away. He enters a second needle into the muscle and asks me to contract it.

'Use all your strength, Kim, as hard as you can.'

He watches the monitor. Another wave appears and then subsides as I relax the muscle.

'Good. Thank you, Kim. You did really well. Angela will take you back to the changing room.'

'When will I get the results?'

'We'll need to collate all the tests, this one together with the bloods we took and the muscle biopsy you're having this afternoon. And there may be further tests. It's hard to say at this point.'

I am in their able hands. I cannot hurry the diagnosis. I must endure the tests and await the outcome as patiently as I can. I imagine it will all end with the conclusion that it's a virus and that I must simply allow it to take its course and, eventually, go.

19

GARY

October 2018

There is a question to be addressed about the land. I want to find an isolated patch of ground, ideally raised up, a knoll perhaps, that is visible over quite a distance. The ladder will have a foundation, of course, a dug hole into which I'll pour concrete. I have yet to decide whether it should stand upright or at an angle. If at an angle, how steep should it be? I can picture it both at about seventy-five degrees to the horizontal and, then again, at forty-five. Or will it be vulnerable at an angle, more likely to be blasted over in a storm? Perhaps a fully upright position will give it greater strength and resilience?

I have changed my mind and decided to explain to Angus the plan I have for Kim's memorial. It's evident now that I must take a certain number of islanders into my confidence if I am to carry this project through to completion.

'You lost your wife six months or so ago, you say?'

'It's nearer eight now.'

To my relief, he's not as curious as I'd feared he might be.

'Where did you have in mind?' he asks.

'I don't know the island well enough to say. The important thing is that it stands out.'

I thought he might know of a piece of land where I could erect it.

'A splendid tribute to your beloved late wife. I understand, Mr Montrose. It's very much to your credit that you want to do this.'

There isn't irony in his remark, is there? Surely, he wouldn't be cruel enough to poke fun at my scheme. But, as his wife testifies, he likes to cavil.

'I suppose my only reservation,' he says, 'is why here. Why on the island? I believe you said you visited the island just once when your wife was alive. She had no real associations with the place. Isn't it a rather odd place to remember her?'

He has a point. I came here, for the most part, to escape memory, to separate myself from the man I was, from Gary, who did what he had to do, but took no pride in it, a man who should perhaps be condemned with sympathy and forgotten. Yet, I am convinced it's right to create the memorial to her here.

'This is where I live now, Angus.'

'But you might move away.'

'That's not my intention. This is where I think of her, where I live with her in my every waking thought. If I'm to make this monument to her, I want to be able to see it, every day if I need to.'

Angus smiles, shyly I think. He is disconcerted by my intensity.

'In that case, you might consider the north of the island.'

Someone has entered the shop. I heard the doorbell ring.

'Mrs Steele!'

Angus acknowledges her with a nod.

She walks around the shelves, heavy overcoat, a woollen hat, a woman who might not have looked out of place shopping here in the nineteen fifties. I don't know Mrs Steele. I've seen her about in the village, but we've not spoken. Her presence inhibits me. I don't want to discuss Kim's memorial in her hearing.

'The north of the island,' Angus continues. 'As I say, the land isn't up to much. It has boggy places, mind, but where there is higher ground, it should suffice.'

'What about ownership?'

Angus removes his glasses and places them on the sales counter. He considers his reply.

'That's possibly a problem. Some of the land up there is old fields and there are disputes going back decades about who owns what. Then, there's some of it for which there are deeds and records of title and such. And, again too, there's parcels of barren mud no one will claim for the rest of time. I imagine you'll have to take pot luck. Pick your spot and see how much of a row ensues.'

In fifteen minutes, I'm back where I was the other day, on the north coast and overlooking a sea that's turbulent and scarred white. Today, however, it makes a different impression. This could be the site of Kim's memorial, her last resting place, as I see it. Is this the right setting? It should be capable of instilling both sadness and joy, continuity as well as loss. If I erect the ladder here, I want to be able to return, time and again, and stand before it and remember Kim. I want to feel free to laugh and to cry, to punch one angry fist into the palm of the other and call on God to justify what He did.

I step out of the Hilux. It's just come on to rain, a fine cold drizzle, fresh in my eyes. I walk towards the cliff. The ground is soggy and poorly drained. It drags on my boots, like a misery that won't go away. The rain gnaws at my hands.

The land rises before it reaches the bluff. As I climb, I make better progress and reach the summit and the cliff edge. I'm aware that it's become drier underfoot. The view down is sheer, a vertiginous wall of shining black rock that drops to ragged boulders doused in surf. Out at sea, the rain and mist shorten visibility. I can just make out the dark, pocket-sized island that stands offshore, uninhabited, lighthoused, protected for its birds, its gannets and oystercatchers.

The bitter rain coarsens my face. I wipe away wet from my eyes with the back of my hand.

Kim relished weather like this, luxuriated in it. If we'd hired a cottage, maybe on a Yorkshire moor, and the rain started to batter the windows and swing in coils around the house, she'd suggest that we went for a hike.

'Wrap up!' she'd say, shout more like. 'Hat, scarf, gloves, walking stick, let's go!'

We'd breast the weather, like athletes, and push on through the rain, hail, sleet, whatever came at us.

'Don't you love it!' she'd say, and throw her arms wide. She'd offer her face to the rain, glory in the wet streaming into her eyes and down her cheeks.

If she slipped in the mud, she'd laugh. I once videoed her as she stepped into a boggy pool and flooded her boots. She yelped and rolled over, giggling.

'Do you want to turn back?'

'You must be joking! We've only just started. It's only water. I'll walk faster. My feet'll warm up soon enough.'

She'd take on ten miles in sodden socks and boots, defying the rain to lessen her happiness.

That seems a long time ago. Standing on this thin crag, dizzy from the drop and the brutality of the rocks below, I wonder about toppling over, flying down to my death. What would it feel like? Have I much more to give?

I miss you, my darling. On some evenings, I yearn for you so much I can't concentrate on anything else. Images on the TV screen pixilate, the shapes of everyday astigmatise. I hold on to the back of a chair for dear life, shaking with loss.

This is not the place. This is not where I can lay you to rest. It is too aggressive.

There is no God, here or anywhere. Why waste my anger on Him? My *fearg*.

20

KIM

April 2011

I'm sure people on the train thought I'd got a screw loose. I couldn't help smiling, broadly, on the brink of laughing out loud. I was so happy, utterly swept away by the news that I was pregnant, and so soon after we'd decided to try. I'd missed my period, and immediately tested myself at home. I knew there was always the chance of getting a false result, but when it came up positive, I felt high as a kite. I could scarcely contain myself, but I didn't tell Gary. I wanted to be certain.

Dr Bruce looked me squarely in the eye.

'No doubt about it, Kim. Congratulations!'

'Oh thank you! Thank you. It's such good news. It means so much to me. To us.'

'Have you told Gary yet?'

'No, but I will tonight.'

'There'll be various monitoring tests, as you go on. We usually send you for an amniocentesis around sixteen weeks.'

'Of course. Better safe.'

I was impatient on the platform, frustrated that the train was delayed. Having withheld the result of the first test from Gary, I couldn't wait to surprise him. He'd be home from work now. I WhatsApped him to make sure there was wine in the fridge.

The train got in around 6.30 and I took a taxi from the

station. Gary was pouring himself a drink when I stepped into the kitchen.

'Hi, sweetheart! Glass of wine?'

'Just a small one, thanks.'

'Not like you.'

'There's a reason. Sit down.'

He returned the bottle to the fridge and pulled out a chair.

'You're not—?'

He took a quick swig of his drink.

'Yes! I'm pregnant.'

'Wow! How many weeks?'

'Four.'

'Wow!'

His response was more muted than I'd hoped for. I suppose if I'd given it any thought and looked back on the last couple of months, I'd have realised that Gary's commitment hadn't measured up to mine. We'd made love passionately enough. He never lacked enthusiasm for that. But whenever we touched on the subject of conception, it had seemed to me that he went along with it, paid lip service, rather than embraced the idea wholeheartedly. I, on the other hand, was fanatical. At my suggestion, we went to bed an hour earlier than usual and had sex every night. I had convinced myself that there was a moment in every couple's routine of lovemaking when fertilisation was uniquely likely. The more frequently we made love, the less risk there was of missing it. Opportunity was all.

Mad, I know, but the urge to conceive can drive you a bit doolally.

'Presumably, it's too early to say if it's a boy or a girl?' Gary said.

'Much. If we want to know, they can usually tell us when I have my ultrasound.'

'When's that?'

'Sixteen to twenty weeks, about the time I have the amniocentesis. The technician has to be able to see the baby's genitals.'

'Is that a problem?'

'Can be.'

Gary was overwhelmed. It was obvious from the questions he was asking me. They didn't seem at all personal. They were the enquiries you made of a distant cousin who was newly pregnant, or a friend you didn't know very well. I imagined his thoughts were in turmoil and, to avoid the awkwardness of silence, he reached for the ready-made, off the shelf questions that didn't, in any way, disclose what he was feeling. I could understand, but I couldn't sympathise. This was supposed to be an adventure we were embarking on together. I wanted him to be eager, excited, alongside me and, instead, it was as if I had him on a long tether, which I was dragging behind me.

'You are pleased, Gary, aren't you?'

'Of course,' he said. 'Why wouldn't I be?'

'Do you realise what a peculiar thing to say that is?'

He had been staring out of the kitchen window, watching a starling stab its beak at the lump of bird feed we had suspended from the windowframe. He now turned to me and shrugged his shoulders.

'How am I meant to react?'

'As if you cared.'

My God, it was a mistake to say that. I don't think I'd intended to. Yes, I was angry with him for failing to rise to the occasion, for behaving as if he were observing me rather than sharing in my joy and supporting me. But I didn't want to hurt him or humiliate him. He stood up, his face flushed with resentment.

'That's what you think?'

He left the room.

I was on the brink of tears. I'd planned it all so well. I'd thought my exuberance would capture him and we'd hug and kiss and toast our baby with our charged glasses. I'd pictured it all on the train, smiling to myself, sweeping through a blur of English countryside. I could see his face over the rim of his glass, thrilled, specks of light in his eyes, mine, exultant.

What now? We hadn't exactly rowed, but we'd certainly crossed, antagonised each other, on the very day and at the very moment when we should have been most intimate. I'd been so stupid to challenge whether he cared. Of course, he cared, but in a way that differed from my expectations, from the caring I demanded of him. It had always been a problem. I knew that deep down, and only reluctantly articulated, he thought he knew me better than I knew myself, knew the weakness I would rather not acknowledge, my impatience, my 'lack of composure', as he liked to call it.

But he didn't.

I could never accept that.

21

GARY

October 2018

I took delivery of forty-five cans of paint yesterday. Each one contains five hundred millilitres. They all have a gloss finish. Angus organised the purchase. Without a credit card, I can buy nothing on the internet and so I depend on him to order what I need. His occasionally cross-grained manner belies a kind personality. He cares about his community. I've come to admire and like Angus over these past few weeks.

The paint cans stand in three rows on the floor of my workshop. Once I'd placed the last, I stood back and admired them. I turned to the ladder, propped up behind the workbench. This feels like a proper project now. I have started.

The ladder will be striped. None of the wood will be visible. I plan to paint two-centimetre stripes along the entire length of both stiles. Each rung, by contrast, will have its own distinct colour. I will then varnish the whole. Two coats probably.

But before I can do all that, I must prepare the whole thing, rungs and stiles, with a primer. I hoick the ladder onto the workbench. It's heavy. I doubt that I'll be able to erect it into position without assistance. I suspect it will take three men, two to hold the ladder, another to shovel cement into the foundation. Angus might help. I will also ask Fraser. That day is weeks away, though. I have the ladder to paint and I've yet to find a suitable site.

Once the primer is dry, the first brush stroke is arbitrary, on a rung picked at random. The paint is tan, the colour of sun-browned skin, Kim's skin through the summer months. Whenever the day allowed, she liked to stretch out on a lounger. She had a lime green bikini she used to wear to show off her tan. She'd walk onto the terrace in bare feet, always red varnish, and unfold the sunbed while I watched at a distance. She knew my eyes were on her, admiring her elegant legs, the shadow between her breasts as she picked up her book and sat down. She'd blow me a kiss, acknowledging my appreciation, and rather than read, she'd shut her eyes against the intense sunlight.

That summer I noticed how her body changed. For years, her stomach had been flat and muscular, sculpted by exercise, but now it grew, gently swelling, little by little, as the baby herself grew and gathered up life. By August, she was frequently uncomfortable, but she insisted on lying out in the sun, turning on one side, then the other, trying to manage the heavy curvature of her belly. She never complained, but I could see in her face that she struggled at times. I helped, if I could, with cushions, cups of tea, fanning her when she was hot, massaging her lower back to ease her bouts of sciatica.

I took my time, cared for her. She'd fall asleep and sometimes she'd surprise me by waking and starting to talk, but with her eyes still closed.

'Are you excited?'

'Of course.'

'No! Not "of course", my darling. Tell me what excites you, what you're expecting, what you're hoping for.'

Her eyes were open now and bright with anticipation. But this was thin ice we were approaching. I knew I had to tread warily. I had learnt, over the weeks and months of her pregnancy, that she was eager to hear what I looked forward to, but it must be a future compatible with the one she envisaged. If I departed from that, intuited her incorrectly, I was told that I was being unreasonable or inadequate.

It was, I found, all too easy to be one or the other.

'I'd be very content with a healthy baby and a safe delivery for you.'

'That's so wet, Gary.' She pushed me away. 'You can do better than that.'

'It's true. That's all that matters.'

'I know! But let your imagination rip a bit!'

I pulled out a chair and sat at the table next to the lounger. The metal of the chair had heated up in the sun. It burnt to the touch.

'I want her to change the world for the good.'

'See! You can do it. Is she a saint?'

'An activist.'

'That's good. I like activist.'

She punched the air, then gripped my hand and squeezed it.

'I want her to be an athlete. I want her to achieve all the ambitions I had as a girl.'

'An activist athlete.'

'What a star!'

She leant forward and kissed me keenly on the mouth.

'Our child will be exceptional,' she said. 'Someone the world looks up to.'

'I hope you're not going to be too demanding a mother.'

'Of course I am. Adrianna will drown in the expectations I have of her.'

She laughed. I took her in my arms and pulled her towards me and held her tightly.

'And you know what Adrianna will say, don't you?'

'No?'

'Don't make a fuss!'

The work on the ladder has progressed well this morning. I have four rungs painted. I plan to be methodical when it comes to painting the stiles, to follow the mathematical sequence I worked out on my laptop. The numbering of each colour ensures that the colours are complementary. I put Burnt Siena next to Pale Gold, violet next to navy. They set each other off superbly. Gloss was undoubtedly the right choice. The rungs gleam in the light from the workshop window.

Do you like it?

I wish for your approval, my love, your forgiveness.

22

KIM

November 2011

Naturally, I knew very little about it. I was consumed with pain. It felt like an aggressive force, invading me, pushing ever deeper, eviscerating me. I thought: my womb, my stomach will never recover from this. This is pain that causes irreparable damage, life-changing injuries.

Was I screaming?

The pain monopolised me, overwhelmed thought. Minutes would pass and I'd be convinced the pain had peaked. Then it would surge again, with renewed strength and violence. My capacity to imagine pain was continuously overthrown by a new possibility, a new magnitude.

A woman approached, a nurse, with kind words.

'You'll be fine, Kim. We're going to give you something for the pain.'

I felt the pressure of her firm hands under my back, turning me, crooking my knees.

'You'll feel a little sore,' she said, 'when the needle's put in.'

I opened my eyes. I wanted to see who the people were who were looking after me.

I felt my lower back become damp as an anaesthetist prepared the area of skin for the needle. I shrank inside.

Lying on my side, curled up, knees close to my chest, I could see the empty part of the room. It was stark, clinical. The grey walls and strip lights offered no comfort, no warmth.

Someone said: 'Placenta possibly?'

Beneath me was a steel bed. The nurse wheeled a drip alongside. I felt like I was in a lab, there to produce some kind of chemical interaction.

They inserted a catheter in my back. The pain persisted in my stomach, but almost immediately my legs went numb. Then, something slow and soft diffused through my waist and abdomen.

'C-section?'

Another voice.

'Too late.'

I was allowed to lie on my back again. There were more people in the room than I remembered. The new faces looked anxious.

I was going under. I could no longer keep my eyes open. I was slipping away, detached from pain, learning the gentle, elegant art of flying.

'....to stop the bleeding,' the voice said.

23

GARY

July 2012

Frankly, it took quite a while to recover. In many ways, we struggled. Kim spent two weeks in hospital. I visited every day. I held her hand and we wept together. I worried that, in her weakness, she would suffer too much from her grief and her hours of tears. I hugged her, appalled by how thin she was, the loss of muscle. I told her we would try again. I told her we would survive, that we would find happiness again.

'We have lost Adrianna,' was all she said.

She had died of placental abruption. When the doctor informed us, I understood nothing of what he said. He failed to elaborate for several minutes and we looked at each other, feeling stupid. Should we have learnt this term in ante-natal classes?

'It's when the placenta separates from the womb.'

'Would she have suffered?' Kim asked. Her eyes were swollen and brimming. I tightened my hand and felt hers diminish in mine.

'The baby experiences significant trauma because it is denied oxygen and nutrients.'

'She!'

'I'm sorry?'

Kim was shouting.

'Our baby was a girl. Adrianna. Don't call her "it".'

'My apologies. I didn't know your baby had a name.'

'Adrianna,' Kim said again.

'Beautiful.'

I said thank you. I don't know why. I suppose there was so very little of Adrianna to hold on to that an acknowledgement of her name, a beautiful name, was better than nothing at all.

Sometimes, sitting on the ward, waiting for Kim to wake up, I would stop breathing. It was as if I'd missed a critical breath and nearly died. It was shocking, terrifying. I choked, convulsed. Whenever it happened, a nurse would rush over to me to see if I was alright. The effect was only ever momentary. I'd thank her and ask for a glass of water.

It happened several times.

I think it was simply grief, the physical assault of outrageous emotions I could not manage. Somehow, God knows how, if I was with Kim, I could contain it, translate it into unexceptional tears. But alone, I lost control. The wave was too big, too vast over my head. I was fighting my way towards the surface, never getting there, endlessly gasping for air, for help.

I brought Kim home on a Monday morning. The hospital had asked me to collect her early, around 8 a.m. She seemed fragile to me, but the ward sister assured me that she was fit enough to be discharged. I drove her through the rush hour. She flinched when a car horn blasted or, once, when an ambulance tore through the line of traffic, blue light sweeping across our windscreen. I could see what a torment it was to her, how she struggled to bear it.

I made breakfast for us in the kitchen. I turned on the radio and landed on *Start the Week*, Andrew Marr leading a discussion on the subject of Civilisation. I couldn't concentrate. It was the sort of conversation I usually liked to listen to, but that day it grated. I wasn't sure whether debate about civilisation dwarfed what Kim and I were going through or that it was the other way around. At any rate, the two were in conflict.

We stumbled through the following days and weeks. We didn't go out unless it was to the supermarket and, generally, I did that. On the whole, we comforted each other, though we didn't sleep well in the same bed and that made us tetchy at times. Neither of us had an appetite, and that combined with the enervating effect of bereavement itself left us vulnerable to illness. Kim developed flu in the third week she was home.

'I'm angry', she said one evening when she was recuperating. 'Some people who lose a loved one experience the presence of the dead person, don't they? I've felt none of that. Adrianna has just gone. I want her back.'

While Kim was away in hospital, I'd removed the baby clothes we had bought and taken them to a charity shop. I'd similarly disposed of the cot and the stroller on e-bay. I now waited for Kim to attack me for removing all trace of our child. Even though her death had denied Adrianna the opportunity to wear the pink and yellow sleepsuits or be scooted along a forest track in her top-of-the-range stroller, I feared Kim would associate all these things, rashly purchased before her birth, with her mourned baby.

But she didn't.

I suppose it's taken several harrowing months, but I have seen a change, in me and in Kim. It's as if Adrianna's death has begun to lose some of its scale, its enormity. I'm starting to grasp what has happened rather than be simply overwhelmed by it. It's a tragedy of such depth and sorrow that I once thought I would never discover any happiness or reward in life again. But that is no longer true. I make a point of ringing Annie, Kim's assistant in the shop, to ask her to deliver flowers twice a week, and Kim is always grateful. She takes obvious pleasure in their bright colours, their miscellaneous scents.

The first tangible sign that she had improved was that she began putting on weight and, at much the same time, taking exercise. She resumed her thrice weekly cycle rides and she went swimming again.

'I think we should go on a hiking holiday,' she announced one day.

It was an idea that came out of the blue, but I was reassured.

'The Highlands,' she added.

24

GARY

October 2018

Like its counterpart in the west, the north-east of the island is sparsely populated. Topographically, though, it's very different. In contrast to the steep promontories that characterise the north-west coast, there are shelves of sloping grassland that descend to white sand beaches. The bay here is flanked by reddish rocks. The sea, at least today, is clear and skirts the sand in a shallow, flat wave.

I've parked the Hilux a short distance from the beach. There's a light breeze and the sun is sparring with a bank of smoky cloud. For once, the day seems reasonably warm. The forecast is, as usual, for rain, but just at the moment it's agreeable, a day that makes you glad to be out. The air is soft.

Ahead of me, at the northern end of the bay, I can see that the land rises, away from the beach and the red rocks. I'd spotted the higher ground on an Ordnance Survey map I'd picked up from Angus the first week I was here. The contour lines tightened a few hundred metres from the coast. I think it's bound to be a small knoll, a *cnocan*. It could well be the site for Kim's memorial.

We visited the island just the once during that Highland holiday. We hired bikes on the mainland and travelled them over on the ferry. We planned to make a day of it, catching the first ferry crossing out, the last back. It was high summer, long hours of daylight.

Kim was in better spirits than I'd anticipated. Ever since she'd proposed going away, she'd kept herself busy and scarcely mentioned the baby. I was the one who brought up the subject and, whenever I did, Kim would skip on to another topic. It was disconcerting at first. In the weeks following Adrianna's death, I had found it difficult to distract her. It had been all, understandably, that she wanted to talk about. It had occupied all thought, all feeling. But now? Impossible to tell. Her apparent recovery might be temporary. Mine too.

As we cycled away from the harbour, I noticed a fisherman in yellow oilskins preparing to take his trawler out to sea. He'd just cast off and was gunning the engine, waiting for the ferry to clear so that he could head out. It was Struan Lamont, of course, but I didn't know that then.

We rode up the hill that takes you through the village and up to what is now my home. Looking back, I realise that that day trip was an informal recce. Perhaps 'unconscious' would be a better word for it. I had no idea at the time that I would ever have need of a bolt-hole and that the island would serve that purpose.

At the post office, we saw a man (Angus) loading a mailbag into his van. He didn't look our way as we swept by, used to cyclists, I supposed. We climbed the grass bank above the cottage and drove on up the west coast. Kim was energetic, strong. I had trouble keeping pace, but I was glad to see her revived, almost as fit as she used to be before the pregnancy. It was uplifting, spurred me on.

'Come on, snail man!'

She'd stopped where the land levelled out and was standing astride the bike. From past cycle rides, I knew that meant a pause, recovery for a few minutes, not a scheduled rest.

'You're not as fit as you should be,' she said.

'Out of practice.'

More than that, I was severely out of breath.

'Look at that!'

We were on the headland with an uninterrupted view across the Irish Sea, sitting under an ash grey sky mottled by sunlight.

'It's breaking through.'

'It's winning!'

'We are, too, aren't we?' she said.

'I think so.'

She jumped off the bike and allowed it to fall to the grass. Before I knew it, she was wrapped around me, clutching me tight, as if she feared to let me go.

'I love you,' she said, with an intensity that I'd not experienced for many months.

We kissed, tender yet eager, reunited, setting a course, I felt. There was a sense in which we had made up after a rift, found our way back to each other when, for a while, we had been travelling on divergent paths. I hadn't realised it. On the contrary, I'd thought that, over these last few months, we were mired in the same slough of despond. But this passion, this hunger, suggested something else. It suggested we had come together from distances apart. We had made, without saying a word beyond love, a new compact, a new bond, the consequence of grief, but promising a future in which joy was possible, an idea that for a long time we had thought incredible.

That night we made love in a B&B on the mainland. The

bed creaked. I rediscovered her body, its delicate slenderness, the beauty of her face in half light. How can I say I'd forgotten what it was like to feel physical love? Surely you don't forget the sensations of making love with a partner you've shared your life with? Yet, that night, it had all the acuity of new experience, the euphoria of feelings not remembered before.

We lay back with held hands. Occasionally, she looked at me, as if she was about to speak.

But she didn't.

Above me, seagulls circle and dive. Do they imagine I have a bag of food, waiting to be thrown in handfuls?

The more I stand here, the more I like this knoll and think it could well be suitable. As soon as I reached the top and saw that it was level, I knew that the shape of it was right. I could easily sink the foundations in the middle of this circular, flat patch of ground. It extends perhaps five metres across. There is space enough, if I want, to create a small terrace with the memorial ladder at its centre.

Having decided on it, I hope I won't be disappointed. I need to establish who, if anyone, owns the land. I pull out my phone and take a few pictures to show people. If there is an owner, what view will he or she take of my project?

Another hurdle.

25

GARY

December 2012

I took her dancing. After Adrianna.

We'd been cooped up in the house. It was Kim's day off and snowing outside, and I knew she was restless. She kept thumbing through magazines without pausing to read anything. She would have been more contented at work.

We decided on the 606 Club in Chelsea. We'd been meaning to go for a while, but hadn't got around to it. The club had been going for forty years, so I suppose we'd felt there was no hurry.

We skidded a couple of times on the way there, and I was relieved when we turned into Lots Road and found a parking space straightaway. We stepped out of the car into a couple of inches of snow, and crossed the road to an arched doorway, which was the club's discreet entrance. Driving by, I'd always thought it must be a real dive. A black painted door made it look as though it ought to be to a safe house or a brothel.

'Who's driving home?'

'Me?' I said.

'Correct.'

She laughed.

'It's fucking cold,' she said.

There was a bell to one side of the door. I pressed it and immediately I heard jazz piano and a voice that said "606".

Before I could reply, a buzzer sounded, a latch clicked and the door opened a few inches.

The jazz was superb, a London quartet at first, covering Miles Davis, then a guitarist from Budapest came on to play Hungarian ethno-jazz.

I tugged Kim on to the dance floor.

'What about another drink first?' she shouted over the band.

'We came here to dance. You can drink later!'

The club was small, most of it occupied by chairs and tables. People ate, drank and listened to music. There was no dance area to speak of. We were the only couple on our feet. No one seemed to mind.

Hungarian ethno-jazz, which I'd never heard of, turned out to be a fusion of hard bop and modern jazz. It suited us just fine and we swayed about the floor, watching each other's moves, excited to be out of the house, active. The music was loud, drums supreme. I took Kim's hand and span her round. She pirouetted on her own and reversed into my arms. I held on to her, crushed her to me.

Another couple had got up. We revolved around each other, exchanging looks, smiles, mutually aroused, exhilarated to be dancing on a Friday night to a band whose music filled the room and roared from the stage so that we couldn't hear each other speak.

'Such amazing fun!'

Kim was shouting in my ear. It hurt.

'Do you want a drink now?' she asked.

The hard bop gave way to a piece that was slower and melodic. I took her in my arms and we drifted around the small dance floor we'd created for ourselves, kissing occasionally. I turned her away from me and pulled her tight into my chest. I kissed the nape of her neck and told her I loved her.

The relaxed tempo, the long, suspended sax, almost lazy drums, made me realise how tired we were. We sat down and ordered drinks.

'What a good idea this was,' Kim said. 'Your idea, of course.'

'Of course.'

We hadn't been out for weeks. That night in the club felt like a liberation. We drank Italian beer and shared a large pizza with a side bowl of coleslaw. There had been evenings like this in the past when I would have felt increasingly apprehensive as time went on, afraid that what had been comfortable and intimate would slip into a serious conversation, possibly about children, that might alter the atmosphere, at worst pilot us towards a row. But I was certain it wouldn't happen that night. Kim was relishing the pleasures of dancing and dining out. She needed to escape, I felt, to try to forget or at least distance herself, and surrender entirely to the moment, to distraction. The 606 was just that, a made to order *distrazione*.

We listened to the music for a while, sipping our Birra Moretti.

'We don't need anyone else, do we?' Kim said.

I smiled, the safer option, excused by the music.

'Just us,' she added.

She laughed and turned back to the band on the stage.

There had been a chance moment in which I might have engaged, asked her what she meant or agreed too readily, and we might have swung off course, but it had passed and I was sure another would not occur.

26

KIM

2nd June 2017

I have been told. After weeks of tests, of uncertainty and denial, I now know. Rather like hearing about a death, my first reaction was disbelief, a powerful sense that a mistake must have been made, that my blood must have been mixed up with someone else's or carelessly contaminated. Perhaps the sample from the biopsy was mislabelled. Could the EMG have lied?

It's been impossible to tell Gary. I didn't even let him know I had the appointment. He'd have wanted to come, support me.

I expect the news will break him. I might be wrong. In some ways, it might come as less of a surprise to him than it was to me. He's been far more concerned about my symptoms than I have. And yet, I know he's been hoping against hope that whatever diagnosis came out of my scans and examinations, it would be trivial, fixable.

So, I have postponed the inevitable. I feel I want to know more before I commit to a confession.

But I had to tell somebody. I couldn't carry the burden of it entirely alone.

I chose Annie. Why not Penny, down the road? Not sure. I guess I felt safer talking to Annie. She's an employee first, of course, but over the ten years we've worked together, respect and compatibility have grown into affection. I don't see her outside of work. Even at Christmas, we confine our celebrations to a lunch at the brasserie three doors away. But we spend eight and a half hours in each other's company most days, and that has been the context for confidences, companionship and a great deal of laughter.

I hesitated, though. I couldn't help going through a miscellany of possible consequences. Not everyone reacts well to learning about another person's illness. Would she know enough about the condition to react at all? What would her first concern be, me or the future of the business and, therefore, her employment?

I did her a disservice.

'Annie, I've got something I'd like to talk about.'

She interrupted the invoice she was completing.

'Of course. Now?'

'It's as good a time as any.'

'Is it a serious matter?' she asked.

She knew from the agitation in my face that it was.

She put her pen down and stood up. The shop was empty. Was it going through her mind that I might want to dismiss her?

'We've no customers,' she said. 'We could shut up and go for a coffee.'

I nodded.

We walked to Café Rouge and found a table for two in the corner by the window. We ordered two cappuccinos. The red of the seats and benches, the doors and the window frames, was an unexpected comfort. It made me feel secure, easier about confiding, a good choice of Annie's.

'You know I've had a couple of falls in the shop recently?'

Annie stirred the froth in her cup, absorbing the sprinkling of chocolate powder.

'Yes, she said, cautiously I thought. 'Nothing I'd particularly noticed, but yes, you slipped over, I remember, on Valentine's Day.'

'And I lost my grip on a vase just before Christmas. Do you remember? The flowers went all over the floor.'

'Yes.' Hesitant again.

'I'm not well, Annie.'

That startled her. From then on, she couldn't take her eyes off me, as if the symptoms of the illness must be visible if she only looked hard enough.

'Is it serious?'

'Pretty serious, yes.'

Why qualify? Why not be honest and say it plainly? Yes. Serious.

'Are they sure?' she asked.

'I have had a whole range of tests and scans, so I think so. I have motor neurone disease. It was a process of elimination. Once they'd ruled out everything else that might fit the symptoms, it was what they were left with.'

'That doesn't sound very scientific.'

'It's how it works with MND. Because it mimics all sorts of other conditions, it takes time to reach a diagnosis.'

'I'm sorry, Kim. I really am. You've told Gary, presumably?'

'No.'

She stretched across the table and gripped my wrists and squeezed them. Her hands seemed so strong, my arms so feeble.

'You must! He's a right to know.'

'Of course, but it's difficult, Annie. There is no hope of

recovery. It'll destroy him.'

'Isn't motor neurone what Stephen Hawking has? You could live for decades.'

'No one understands why Stephen Hawking has survived for as long as he has. Some people doubt that he has it. Usually, people die within two years or so of when it started.'

'Two years from now?'

'From when I first developed the disease. They can't say for sure when that was.'

'It can't be that long. You've only had symptoms very recently.'

'They can't say, Annie. It could have been a-symptomatic for quite a while before I felt anything was wrong.'

She was trying to give me hope, to find the flaw in the forecast, the anomaly in what had been said to me that would allow me to live a few extra months.

'Are you sure there's no cure? They discover things all the time.'

'You're not listening, Annie. There is no cure and not much they can do to slow down the disease or alleviate the symptoms. It's shit, frankly.'

She sat back and I realised she was now at a loss what to say. She sipped her cappuccino, returned it to the table. She looked down at it, as if it were tea leaves and she might divine a better future.

'I'm sorry to be the bearer of bad news,' I said. I felt oddly guilty.

'No, no, it's fine. Don't worry about me. I'm sorry for you. It's terrible.'

This had been a moment of recognition for me. For as long

as I had kept the diagnosis to myself, I could entertain the possibility of error. Motor neurone disease, the condition, had an unreality about it. It had yet to be objectively true. But as I talked with Annie, as I had, more and more, to refute her optimism, her conviction that my life expectancy must be longer than doctors had predicted, that medical science must, in the nature of its miraculous advancement, come up with an answer, I realised there was no remedy awaiting me, no saving slip-up that led to the wrong opinion being given.

'I'm afraid I'm stuck with it.'

'But you can fight it!' she said.

27

GARY

November 2018

It turns out that the plot of land I've identified as a possible site for Kim's memorial belongs to Struan Lamont. Years ago, there was a small croft there, which passed down the generations, less and less agriculturally viable in each, until it reached Struan. I saw no sign of anyone farming when I was up there last week, and the buildings, such as they were, amounted to fragments of two low stone walls.

'You'll take tea?'

He'd steered me towards a chair at his kitchen table.

'Wee bit early for a dram, wouldn't you say?'

'Tea would be lovely.'

The sun streams through his window on to a table crowded with newspapers and tins of flies and bait. The tins sparkle in the light.

'You didn't say very much on the phone, Mr Montrose,' he says.

'No, I thought it would be better to meet. Look, call me Greg, if you like.'

'Aye, well we might be a few months off that, I suspect.'

He presents me with a mug of dark tea, the face of a young Queen Elizabeth on thick white china. He sits facing me and sweeps away the tins to make room for his own mug. His has a wide panorama of mountains and the word AVIEMORE in large capitals underneath.

'Tell me what's on your mind,' he says.

I hesitate. There's part of me that thinks my proposed memorial, or at least the form it will take, is a bit unhinged, so I'm uncertain how Struan Lamont will react.

'You know that my wife passed away?'

'I had heard. I'm sorry for your loss.'

'Yes. Thank you. It's getting on for eight months now. I gather you lost your wife.'

'Aye, but that's a long while in the past.'

He's put it behind him. We are not going to discuss it, at least not yet.

'I want to create a memorial to Kim, my wife.'

'An admirable gesture.'

He raises his mug and nudges it in my direction, gaps in his teeth as he smiles.

'The thing is I want to erect it somewhere on the island where it can be seen at a distance. From the land and out at sea. I want it to be visible to passing boats.'

'Do I gather you're referring to that wretched strip of godless land I own on the north coast?'

'It's not that bad.'

I show him the photos I took on my phone.

'Even by the standards of this island, it's bleak. It's a miserable place, man. Why would you choose it?'

I'm taken aback. My fear had been that he might be fond of the plot, might love its isolation, the magnificence I discovered in it. It had never occurred to me that he would see it as repugnant.

'Beauty in the eye of the beholder and all that.'

'That I can't believe. Beauty! The whole area is utterly cheerless. It's just bog and rock.'

'The bay is beautiful.'

'You won't get a tree to grow there, let alone a potato. They haven't farmed it for two centuries. I don't suppose it gave out much then.'

'Fortunately, I don't need to grow anything. Would you be willing to give me your permission to put up my ladder there?'

'Ladder?'

'I'm sorry. I should have explained. The memorial is a painted ladder. My wife was a florist. She loved colour, bright colours, vivid combinations. So, I'm painting a ladder in forty-five different shades. That was her age, you see, when she died. She'd love it, I think.'

'How will it stand up? The weather is rough up there.'

'The lower rungs will sit in a concrete base.'

'You'll forgive me, Mr Montrose, when I say that people up here will say you're *seòlta*. You've gone crazy.'

'That's something I'll have to live with.'

'Aye, and you'll be in good company. There's plenty on this isle with a few screws loose.'

'Do I have your permission then?'

'How much will you give me for it? It's a permanent rental you're after?'

Struan Lamont sits back on his chair and waits. He drinks his tea and stares across the table at me. I don't know what to suggest. Does he expect very much, given how much he detests the place? I start to speak and he immediately interrupts.

'No! Only joking. It's a worthless piece of shite! You're

welcome to what you want.'

'That's very good of you. Thank you.'

'I should probably have done something of the kind in memory of my own wife.'

'How long ago did she die?'

I realise I'm putting our agreement at risk. Perhaps the question is intrusive. But I feel I can't ignore the subject altogether. She must have been quite young when she developed the cancer.

'Twelve years. Cancer of the bowel.'

'Did she have it for long?'

Do I tell him more about you, Kim? I think not. I don't want to invite comparisons and judging by the way he veered away soon after I arrived, Struan doesn't either.

'We went through two and half years of hell, if that's what you mean. She'd presumably had it for some while before all that started. She wasn't able to do much for herself for most of that time, and the last few months, nothing.'

'You were her carer?'

'I did everything. Cook, bottle washer, nappy changer. I had to pull the boat out. Lived on hand-outs. But it was worth it.'

'Worth it?'

I've said it before I have time to consider what I'm saying. Struan looks agitated, as if I've challenged his values, the propriety of his care for his wife. I decide to apologise.

'Yes, it was worth it, Mr Montrose. Every day that I washed my Ishbel and fed her and dressed her and undressed her and took her to the toilet and wiped her arse, every day that I did that, I loved her a little more. And she, that brave woman, endured it all.'

'Exhausting for you.'

'I did it willing. You went through something not dissimilar, I gather.'

'For not as long.'

'But you understand. More than most.'

'Yes, perhaps. You must have reached a point when she would rather have died.'

Struan is on his feet, running water into a kettle. He places the kettle on the hob and turns to me.

'We never considered an alternative. It didn't accord with our beliefs. This life is a lottery, as you well know, Mr Montrose. There's those who live into their nineties, free of any problem, downcast when they have a head cold. And then there's others struck down as children or toxic with cancer in mid-life. There's nothing any of us can do about it.'

'I meant that you must have wished....at times, you must have wished to shorten her suffering?'

'How might we have done that?'

I want to answer him, to touch on the thorny issue, but he is evidently hostile to it. I can see in his face that, in his wife's case, he not only disapproved of the idea, but suspects me of holding the opposite view and wants to deny me any moral right to it. I have to lie.

'I don't know,' I say. 'People go to Switzerland.'

'It's not for us to decide, though, is it?'

'You think it's in the hands of God?'

'That would be it.'

He places a second mug of tea in front of me and removes the teaspoon he's been stirring it with. It drips on the newspapers. I watch a dark pool spread over the photographed face of a missing woman.

'Who is to say what His plan was, why my Ishbel could not be saved her anguish? No, there's no knowing. But there are laws for good reasons, aren't there? She had to endure, and I had to care for her without stint or distaste. That was my duty, any husband's duty. Would you not agree, Mr Montrose?'

Mr Montrose. Again and again. I notice that he uses it now to accuse me, but of what? Contradiction? Dishonesty? Lack of love?

'It can break your heart to watch another human being in agony.'

'Indeed, it can. Then we agree.'

'Have we disagreed?' I ask.

'I have a sense that you are holding back.'

Am I? Would I rather confess that we did speak about the alternative, Kim and I, that we considered what we called 'the Swiss Option'? Not that we planned to go there, to Switzerland, but the euphemism eased the discussion, made it less painful. Am I frightened to engage with Struan Lamont, to argue my case? I like to think I am using my judgement, not giving in to fear.

'No, I'm not, Struan. I'm just conscious of different points of view on this.'

'You are a liberal, are you not, Mr Montrose? A house of many mansions. A phrase from the Authorised Version, very much misunderstood in our times, don't you think? In the days of our king, James VI, a mansion was a room. There are many rooms in your house, I believe.'

His tone has softened. He wants, I suspect, to tidy up our differences and draw the conversation to a close. I anticipate him.

'Well, thank you, Struan. Thanks for giving me permission to use your land, and for the tea, and the stimulating chat.'

'It's been my pleasure to see you, Mr Montrose. Good luck with creating your memorial. Scarcely ever has a ladder been put to a more sublime use.'

28

KIM

7th June 2017

That night, I drove home from the shop later than usual. Annie and I had had another chat after we closed. She'd persuaded me that I had to tell Gary about my diagnosis and I was fully intending to.

When I pulled up in the drive, there was no sign of his car and, inside, the house was empty. Then I remembered. Squash night. How could I have forgotten? Every Wednesday he played squash and then, to counteract any possible health benefit from the game, he went for a beer or two.

The house intimidated me. I needed company, and there was none. I poured myself a glass of wine and hunted through the crowded fridge for something to eat. I found an unopened pizza and switched on the oven.

I drank the wine and gave myself a second glass. It did the trick. I felt my body begin to unwind and the house became a little more friendly. I put the radio on. They were half-way through *The Moral Maze*. Michael Buerk was sounding quite shirty with one of the panellists.

I knew what I was trying to do was avoid thinking about it. The wine, the radio: they were tactics of evasion. But the problem was too big to be pushed aside.

I was determined to beat it. Having said that, I didn't know exactly what I was in for. It was a wasting disease. That much was evident. I had only to look at the photographs of Stephen Hawking to confirm that. But how quickly would it happen? It seemed to me that if I was going to lose musculature, exercise must delay the process of decline. So, I should work out every day from now on. For as long as I could, I'd walk, swim or cycle early in the morning before work. Perhaps I should join a gym and use the weights there, or a rowing machine. I was excited. The prospect of taking remedial action, of staving off the disease through sheer effort, was oddly thrilling. For the first time since I'd accepted the diagnosis, I felt that the battle wasn't lost, that some of the power was in my hands.

It deserved another glass.

I took out the pizza and ate it in front of the TV. There was nothing on that I was particularly interested in, so I watched a repeat of Tim and Pru, those venerable actors, taking one of their canal journeys. Timothy West's gentle, sympathetic voice was comforting, the passage of their narrowboat along the canal and through the locks palliative. They appeared to inhabit a soft, green world. It was tranquil, contented. I wanted to be there.

I must have dozed off. When I woke, it was just after ten. Gary still wasn't home. There was another hour until closing time, so why should he be? I knew I couldn't tell him that night. It was too late.

Half the pizza was uneaten and cold.

My confidence had ebbed, slipped out of the room. I felt uncovered, chilly even, as if a blanket had been snatched away while I slept. The question I usually suppressed surfaced. Why me?

What was I going to do? I felt suddenly lonely. I wanted to cry. Gary would support me. I knew that. He would be utterly dependable. But even he, good old Gary, couldn't save me, could he? All very well to be determined, to plan exercise routines, to refuse to give in to the disease, but they'd said there was no cure and that I must prepare myself for what was to come.

What was that future? How awful would it be? In front of me, on television, there were horrific pictures of wounded patients in a hospital in Syria, hit by missiles only a couple of hours earlier, since I'd come home, images of pure horror. I couldn't compare myself with that, surely? Whatever lay ahead, it had to be better than that.

29

GARY

November 2018

I have unlidded all forty-five cans of paint. They sit on the workshop floor in three rows, bloated Smarties in window light.

I am starting on the stiles. This is a tricky task. I have slightly changed my plan and I've decided that each ring of colour should be a five-centimetre band. I spent part of last night numbering each paint tin and reminding myself of the sequences I'd devised to avoid repetition. In principle, it shouldn't be necessary to paint the lower part of the ladder because it will be buried in concrete, but sentimentally I feel that is cheating. I want to see my tribute to Kim fully completed. When I visit the site, I want to know that the ladder is bright with colour to its feet.

It's a slow business. I have pencilled boundary lines for the painted bands the length of the two stiles. I can now apply an initial coat, which may be all that's required. We'll see. The first paint is *Purple Pout*. This will be the top ring on the left-hand side. I'll then paint the right-hand band in *Volcanic Red*, and allow both to dry. I can then add *Kiwi Crush* and *Sapphire Salute*, and wait for those to dry too. Painting the entire ladder will be the work of several days. But there is no urgency. It is a token of love. I will take my time.

Would you laugh if you could see all this? Would you say that I was ridiculous? I want you to be thrilled by it, long to see it finished. It's unique, after all.

The purple and the red catch the window light, trapping it in crescent-shaped pools. I stand back to admire the concentration of colour. Like good wine, there is depth to it, a richness that I hope doesn't fade too much when the ladder suffers the storms of the north coast.

Someone has knocked on the workshop door. It throws me. People don't call on me, or if they do, as Angus has to when he has a parcel to deliver, they ring the front doorbell. Perhaps that's already been tried.

When I open the door, there is a woman standing in the courtyard. She's a cyclist, quite tall, fifties, I'm guessing. She holds her bike next to her, hands on handlebars. She looks lost. It might be that she needs directions, but more than that, she appears bewildered.

'Gary!'

'Sorry—?'

I don't recognize her.

'Sally. I'm a friend of your wife's.' She leans her bike against the wall of the workshop and comes towards me, hand outstretched. 'Kim and I used to belong to the same cycling club. I met you at the Dobbs' a couple of years ago. New Year's Eve.'

She shakes my hand vigorously. I have no choice but to ask her in.

'I had no idea that you'd moved up here. Or is it a holiday retreat?'

'How did you find out where I live?'

I vaguely remember her face, but would never have put a name to it. The New Year's party must have been the one when Kim collapsed. I'm much more anxious that she has traced me to the island than that she clearly has no knowledge of Kim's death. What's prompted her to look for us, me?

'Gary, I was just as astonished to see you when you opened that door as you were to see me.'

We are standing by the open cans of paint, awkward. I suggest we move to the house. She talks as we walk across the courtyard.

'I've been cycling round the island all morning and I climbed up your hill there and lost the cycle path.'

'Easily missed.'

'Is it? That's a relief. I thought I was just being bloody silly about it.'

'No, no.'

I guide her through the back door.

'I called in on you because I thought you might know where it goes. Except that I didn't know it would be you living here, of course. How are you both? Where's Kim?'

We sit in the kitchen. I'm restless, put out.

'You obviously didn't hear at the time. Kim passed away. Just over eight months.'

'Oh, Gary! I'm so sorry. She was always so fit. What a stupid thing to say! Sorry. What happened?'

This is an eccentric conversation, I feel. A woman I scarcely know has inadvertently tracked me down to an island off the west coast of Scotland and sits in my house enquiring about the cause of my late wife's death several months ago. She is in tears, and I find myself curiously unsympathetic. Her grief seems to me an imposition. I have been coping well, I think. There are days when the loss is acute, the memories too lifelike, but generally I manage. This woman, Sally, threatens to disrupt that. She unsettles me.

'She developed motor neurone disease,' I explain. 'Started with falls. You might remember she had a fall at that party. So we sent her for tests.'

'Isn't that what Stephen Hawkins had?'

'Hawking. Yes. What everyone says.'

Interminably.

'It must have been awful,' she says. 'For you both.'

'It was cruel, Sally. That's my view. No human being should have to endure the kind of physical torment she went through.'

'No. You're right. Especially someone as gorgeous as Kim.'

'No one should have to experience it.'

'Of course! Sorry.'

In less than half an hour, we have progressed from a casual encounter between two people who know each other very slightly to an intense conversation that I can hardly tolerate. I want her to leave, but she shows no sign of doing so and I am so het up I can't think of an excuse to throw her out.

'So, you came up here to escape the memories, I imagine?'

'Kind of. I couldn't continue in our house.'

'No, of course.

'It was filled with her life, everywhere I looked.'

'Naturally. Has it worked?'

'Has what worked?'

'Coming up here.'

For a moment, she interests me. Everything else she has said has aggravated or upset me, but this question is intriguing, chiefly because I haven't asked it of myself. I've gazed in the mirror and seen the blood and my transgression, but I've never reflected on whether or not being here has been a success.

Before I can answer, the doorbell rings.

Angus stands on the lower step and hands over a brown paper bag.

'Thought I'd save you the trouble of coming down,' he says. 'Half a dozen, as ordered. They came in this morning.'

'Thanks, Angus.'

'Sprucing the place up?' Sally asks.

She has stepped behind my shoulder, seen the paintbrushes in the bag. She greets Angus with a nod. I hesitate how to describe her.

'Angus, this is an old acquaintance-friend, Sally. Just visiting the island.'

'I had no idea Gary was living here,' she adds.

Gary. Has Angus noticed? Nothing registers on his face. Does he think it's an easy mistake to make, Gary for Greg? Is it an error a friend would make, though?

'Pleased to meet you, Sally,' he says.

'We haven't seen each other for a couple of years,' I explain. 'Sally was a friend of my late wife's.'

'I didn't know,' Sally says.

Angus must be wondering how close a friend Sally is, if she has taken so long to find out that Kim is dead. Will it allow him to excuse her confusion over my name? I hurry the conversation to a close.

'We mustn't detain you, Angus. Thanks again. They'll be put to good use.'

'No bother, Mr Montrose. Glad to be of service.'

He is stepping down into his van. Sally waves as he leaves.

'Changed your name by deed poll?' she says, once Angus's van is safely beyond the cottage gate.

I try to look puzzled.

'Sorry?'

'Montrose. He called you Mr Montrose.'

'Did he? I didn't notice.' I laugh. 'I suppose a couple of months isn't long enough to register. He'll get it right one day.'

She appears to accept my interpretation and gathers up her gloves from the kitchen table. Should I offer her lunch? What would we talk about? Memories of Kim? I couldn't bear it.

'I'd better be going myself,' she says. 'Can't take up any more of your time, can we? You've got decorating to do.'

We cross the courtyard to where she left her bike. She swings a leg over the crossbar and stands astride it, as Kim used to do. I think she is waiting for something, or it might be that she expects me to kiss her. I lean forward just as she starts to speak. The misunderstanding is awkward.

'I know we don't know each other very well,' she says. 'But I like you, Gary, and Kim was a fantastic woman. So, I want you to know I understand how much pain you must have been through together, and now as you're alone. I really do.'

'Thank you, Sally.'

'I mean it, Gary.'

'Of course. Thanks.'

'Shall I leave you my card? It's got my email and mobile. Don't hesitate to get in touch, if you want to.'

She bites off her glove and pulls out a green wallet from her jeans. She unzips it and takes a card from one of the leather slots and hands it to me.

'Any time, Gary. She was a good friend to me years ago.'

The moment to kiss arrives and I bend forward and brush my lips across one of her cheeks, then the other. It is perfunctory. I'm grateful to her for the affection she once had for Kim, but I can feel nothing kindly for this woman here and now. If anything, she makes me feel guilty.

'If you get to the top of the cliff, keep the coast on your right and you'll rejoin the cycle path.'

She nods her thanks.

I step back into the workshop, as she cycles out of the courtyard, and close the door.

That night I drank. I dropped by the stores in the late afternoon and picked up a bottle of Talisker. Angus made no reference to the morning, so I assumed he'd taken *Gary* to be a simple error, not worthy of mention. Instead, he asked me what I was doing drinking whisky from the south.

'Isle of Skye, isn't it?'

'It is, and run by too large an outfit,' he said.

'The owners, you mean?'

'Diageo! What kind of name would you say that was? Spanish, would it be?'

'English. It's made up. By an agency in London, I think.'

'Well, there you are.'

He sighed and passed the bottle across the counter.

I sat in the front room, a standard lamp behind the chair the only light. The whisky glowed amber. I'd already had two, large ones. That's why I was staring into my glass. You only take to studying the colour of whisky once you've had a couple.

I miss you, Kim. I ache for you sometimes. I had plenty of time to get used to the idea, didn't I? For several months we prepared for your death and I, perhaps hour by hour, adapted to the idea that I was gradually losing you, first to the disease, eventually to death itself. Anticipatory grief, they call it, a series of rehearsals for the final event that supposedly attenuates bereavement, the anguish that, all the same, rushes in the moment breathing stops.

Did I believe it? Yes, it helped. The foreknowledge, the choking outbursts, the shouting, the hammering on the steering wheel of my car: they all helped let it out, coached me for the inevitable. I suppose I was grateful to have the time to be reconciled and, yes, it hurt a little less at the end.

And yet it didn't. Not really. I'm confused. I cried less than I might otherwise have done. I say that! How do I know? Maybe I'd have been the same if she'd died suddenly. I can't say.

What I do know is that there are occasions when your death might just as well have happened yesterday. Like this morning, for God's sake! I was painting the sixth band on the right-hand stile – *Honey Mustard* it was called – and I just had to stop. I was suddenly aware that I was short of breath, and frightened, frightened that my next breath might be my last. I was panicking. I thought it might be a heart attack. Then the shortness of breath, the panic, began to resolve into a single feeling of unbearable loneliness. It was as if I couldn't go on. I wanted you back so badly, Kim, I couldn't hold the paintbrush steady. I was trembling. I put the brush down and gave in to what seemed like a long, slow fit of uncontrollable shaking that went on and on. My breathing came in rough snatches and coughs. I couldn't cry, but my shoulders heaved.

I gripped the workbench and pleaded. Or would you say it was a prayer? I'm not sure what I'm asking for anymore. Is it release? Forgiveness?

My arms shook as I steadied myself on the bench. When will this end? Even eight months on, when days and weeks go by during which I'm assured and confident that I have moved on, I can be caught out, without warning, laid bare, stripped of resilience and dignity. I am forced to see that a door I had thought shut is, in fact, wide open. I am face down in its draught, prone to agony, weak as her wasted arms, fragile as thin glass.

Is this what remains? Should I look forward to a future of superficial acceptance vitiated by attacks of such wilting grief they bring me to my knees?

Kim, you have to forgive me. Please!

30

GARY

August 2014

Two years after Adrianna's death, we tried for another baby. It's hard to remember now, but I suppose we gave it about six months, without success. One evening in the autumn, we talked about adoption. We were in what we grandly called the Laundry – a box room that led off the kitchen – and hanging up wet washing on the dryer. Kim worked at twice the speed I did, athletic, driven by energy.

'There are so many children in need of a home,' I said. 'It would be a kind thing to do.'

She paired blue socks and draped them over the dryer.

'I haven't closed my mind to it, Gary,' she said. 'I'm sure I could love a child I hadn't given birth to. It's not that. It's an emotional thing, isn't it? Adopting just doesn't feel right after Adrianna. Not yet.'

Her unclosed mind should have been the prelude to further discussion, but it never happened. As I watched her hang clothes and snap straight the legs of jeans, I thought we'd dropped the subject only to return to it another day, another chance hour of shared time, shared effort, when it would simply come up. But the moment never arose.

She worked in silence, folding to the basket of clothes in a single, fluid action, bent at the waist, legs straight, her jumper lifted a few inches, her taut waist naked. And when she returned to full height, her arms laden, she did so with a sudden spring, as if released. She raised her arms to the dryer, hooked the sleeves of a yellow top over one of the bars, her fingers quick to do it, dextrous. She became conscious of me watching her.

'Why are you looking at me like that?' she asked.

'Just admiring your body,' I said. 'You do everything with such agility. And you're so graceful.'

'Don't be ridiculous, Gary! I'm hanging up the washing, for God's sake!'

'All the same.'

Each of her movements had a precision and flow to it. She wasn't aware of her own skill. It wasn't planned. She didn't instruct her body. But the beauty of the mechanism, the parts working together, engrossed me.

Always.

31

KIM

8th June 2017

'Did you tell him?'

I can't face her. We're on opposite sides of the shop, making up orders for customers. I am composing a tall arrangement of Moonstone roses, purple sea holly and white Delphinium, the last shooting up from the display like sentinels. I try to find comfort, distraction, in their colours, their mingling perfumes.

'No.'

'Kim, for goodness sake, why not?'

'I meant to. Last night.'

I stand back. It needs another stem or two of green Eucalyptus. I hunt around the buckets on the floor until I find a dozen of them.

'So why didn't it happen?'

'I'd forgotten it was Gary's night playing squash. They go to the pub afterwards, and he didn't come home until after midnight. I don't know. It was too late. And I wasn't going to tell him when he was drunk.'

'Was he drunk?'

'A bit.'

The guy who'd ordered the flowers had left it up to me what to include and how to arrange it. He said he wanted something 'a bit different' and 'modern'. In my view, he looked deeply conservative when he came into the shop, camel coat and a striped tie. I wondered whether he would approve of my idea, which he might think too 'modern', too spiky.

'Are you afraid to tell him?'

I stop what I am doing. I know I've been tweaking the arrangement unnecessarily, lifting and swapping the flowers around in order to avoid engaging with Annie. I walk across the shop.

'Wouldn't you be?'

I've startled her. She's not anticipated having this conversation face to face.

'I don't know,' she says. 'I've never been married.'

'That's not the point.'

'Perhaps not. I suppose I mean I don't know what your Gary is really like, how he'd take it.'

'And you think I do!'

She's infuriated me. I make tea to mute the heated words I'm in danger of voicing. Does she imagine that confiding my illness to Gary will be like admitting to a speeding fine or burnt toast? I know what Gary is like, but nothing in the past has prepared him, or me, for what I must eventually tell him. How can I predict the reactions of a man who learns that his marriage is about to be destroyed, that his wife will soon change out of all recognition and die? Nothing resembles that. There are no comparisons. Even the loss of Adrianna, excruciating in its brutality, was an event we witnessed. We saw what happened together. We went through it together. It wasn't reported to us as an experience to suffer in the future.

I manage to hand Annie her mug without spilling it. She

accepts it with a look I suspect is sorry, seeking forgiveness, but I'm too angry to let her get away with it.

She realises she will have to speak her apology.

'It was thoughtless of me. It must be very difficult.'

'Understatement of the century!'

'What will you do?'

'Take my time, I think. There's never going to be a right moment, is there? But some are worse than others.'

'You know I'm always around, if you—'

'If I what, Anne?'

'Don't bite my head off! I'm trying to help.'

Now it is her turn to feel injured, and I can't blame her. I've been scratchy all morning. Before coming to work, I'd gone on a bike ride for an hour and then I was in the shower at home and I kept dropping the bar of soap. I found it so frustrating, I lost all patience with it. I ended up throwing the soap out of the shower, which was ridiculous. I couldn't continue washing, but I was annoyed with myself for being so clumsy, so helpless to behave in any other way. It corroded my mind and I couldn't shake off the anger. It stayed with me as I cycled to the shop.

'I thought you might like to discuss what you're going to say to Gary, your approach.'

God, she's sweet! I shouldn't shout at her.

'That's kind, Annie. To be honest, I don't know if that would help. Every time I work out in my mind what I'm going to say, it vanishes. Or I remember a few hours later and I can't believe what I was thinking. How on earth could I have thought that was the right thing to say? Mad!'

'Perhaps you shouldn't write it in your head. Perhaps you should just come out with it.'

I hold my mug in both hands. The warmth is comforting. My hands feel stronger now. I don't think I need have worried about dropping it.

'Maybe.'

'Have you got anything planned?'

'What do you mean?'

The shop doorbell rings. Someone has come in.

'A night out,' Annie says. 'Dinner somewhere.'

A woman in jeans and a grey Berghaus jacket smiles at us, inviting help.

'I have a funeral coming up,' she says.

Annie is still looking at me. She shrugs her shoulders.

'Might be an idea, a place you could talk.'

The Chapter was our favoured restaurant. We recommended it to everyone. Oddly, it wasn't in the most attractive part of town, and stood on the other side of the street from a hospital. Gary and I used to joke that if we developed food poisoning or drank ourselves into a stupor, we could always stumble over the road for help.

We loved the décor. Light oak floors, white panelled walls, a sequence of discrete rooms that allowed you to think that you were in a private dining room, yet part of a community. The rooms flowed, one to the next. We had a table at the window overlooking the hospital. It was a large bay with sash windows, and it was raining again outside.

Behind us the wall separating us from the next dining room was hung with old, black and white photographs of what our area looked like in Victorian and Edwardian times. They fascinated me. Horses and carts trundled up the hill towards an impressive spire. Ex-servicemen and boy scouts paraded to church on a Sunday. All the men and women wore hats, sported sticks and umbrellas. Shop fronts had awnings and bold, capital declarations of what they sold: GROCERY & PROVISIONS, CLOTHIER & HATTER, MAC FISHERIES, even BILLIARDS. The manager and staff of the Kosmos Kinema stood in front of their picture house, stiff and grim, awaiting completion of their photograph. One pub had a banner stretched across the first storey. THE TOAST GENTLEMEN – THE QUEEN – GOD BLESS HER. I guessed it dated from 1887 or 1897, one of Victoria's jubilees.

I found these pictures of the past, over a century old, strangely moving. Of course, there was the poignant awareness of wars not yet fought and lives that would end, and perhaps it was that displaced foreknowledge that many of those I was looking at would die young that I found so affecting. Contained in these photographs were lives blessed and lives blighted, the lottery of life summed up. There were young women who would become old maids, boys who would not reach their teens, men who would survive the trenches and, shortly after, die of flu. I wondered whether in the four decades I had trod this earth someone had caught an image of me, in some random street, walking to school, shopping for jeans, dismounting my bike, drawing cash from an ATM, holding my husband's hand. Might I end up on the wall of a restaurant, the only public memory that I'd lived?

I ordered English Asparagus with Poached Duck Egg, followed by Haunch of Venison with cumin and carrot purée, roasted carrots and a hazelnut crust. I forget what Gary had, but he asked them to bring us a bottle of the house white. I was desperate for a glass to calm me down.

'I have something to tell you,' I said.

'That sounds ominous.'

The sommelier was still at the table. He'd invited Gary to taste the wine. Gary performed his usual routine of smelling it, pretending he could detect, I don't know what, gooseberries, fresh grass cuttings. Then he savoured it in his mouth and decided it was good, as if he could tell. The sommelier served us both, planted the bottle in an ice bucket a short distance from the table and left.

'You were saying?'

Gary raised his wine and expected me to do the same. Our glasses touched.

'To us!' he said.

'They've come up with a diagnosis,' I said, a bit more abruptly than I'd intended.

He was shocked. We had been waiting for test results from the hospital for weeks, but I think he hadn't expected that I would choose that occasion, that setting, to give him the news.

'What do they say?'

How could I answer him? I knew I had to. It was why I'd started the conversation. But the burden of knowing that I was about to destroy his happiness, all his hope of contentment in the future, was excruciating. I couldn't bear the possibility of him breaking down in front of me.

I simply came out with it.

'I have motor neurone disease.'

'Christ!'

He stared at me, as if I'd lied to him or revealed that I was having an affair. His face had disbelief all over it, but also hurt.

I felt I'd injured him, stabbed him.

He took his time to reply.

'Are you sure?' he said, eventually.

'Apparently, they can't be one hundred per cent, but they don't have any doubts now. They've ruled out everything else.'

'Everything else that fits the symptoms?'

'Yup.'

He went silent. In some ways, that was worse than the outburst I'd anticipated. I tried to make light of it.

'Please don't mention Stephen Hawking.'

'No, no, of course not.'

He'd taken me seriously.

The asparagus arrived. I could scarcely bring myself to eat. It had been a mistake to think I could disclose something as momentous and life-changing as this over a meal. Gary was numbed by what I'd told him. He kept interrupting his food to return to me, about to speak, then unable to.

'Say something, Gary, please.'

'I'm sorry. It must be so difficult for you, too. I suppose I'm just stunned.'

'It's a lot to take in.'

I didn't resent the way in which he was responding, but I was conscious that I would have to nurse him through the impact of the diagnosis. He was preoccupied with what he felt. I knew it would take several hours, perhaps days, before he began to consider what I was going through, what I was feeling.

'Did they tell you what to expect?' he asked.

'I don't want to go into that now, not here.'

'No. I understand. I know that there's no cure as such, but presumably there's a lot they can do to retard the progress of the disease?'

This was a straw I'd clutched to for a while. Before it snapped. Having made one mistake in choosing to break the news at The Chapter, I decided I wouldn't make a second and deprive him of this single hope, his trust in the NHS, his faith in the idea that when a disastrous outcome is feared, it usually turns out to be not as bad as anticipated.

'We'll see,' I said.

'I don't mean just drugs. Exercise. They'll probably give you a routine to follow every day, to keep you active. We'll get you through this, Kim. I promise.'

Would *we*? I looked at him and realised again how much I loved him. He would support me. I had no reservations or doubts about that. He was a good man, a good husband, ludicrously devoted to me. In every practical way, he would help me. When I couldn't stand, he'd lift me. When I couldn't eat, he'd feed me.

The haunch of venison was enormous. The smell of it sharpened my appetite a little. It was perfectly cooked, tender, juicy, slid apart when I started to cut into it. I made a forkful of meat and combined it with the purée and hazelnut. It was delicious, melt in the mouth rich and succulent. I couldn't imagine eating more than a quarter of what was on my plate.

'Good?' Gary asked.

'Very.'

We had, without voicing it, turned a corner, decided that at least we could enjoy the meal. We drank our wine, savoured our food so far as our appetites would allow. The acute moment had passed. We had, as it were, re-entered the restaurant, become familiar again with our fellow diners, the waiting staff, the

Victorian photographs on the wall, the gentle rainfall outside.

How would he deal with it emotionally? How would he cope with my disintegration, my withering on the vine, my shrinking from view? Yes, I would fight it, every inch of the way. I had the advantage of my impatience, my energy, my absence of fear. But if Gary was to give it his best shot, what would that mean? Would he find a well of resilience he hadn't known was there? Would he set his face against it, hold up his smile for my sake?

'The rain has stopped,' he said.

'Oh, yes.' I hadn't noticed.

We raised our glasses a second time.

'To us!' he said again.

PART TWO

32

KIM

4th November 2017

Gary and I had an interesting conversation this evening. Because I have to sit much of the time, we've taken to playing cards and board games of different kinds, Monopoly, Scrabble, Canasta, that sort of thing. We started doing this because I was watching far too much television, programmes in which I had zero interest. Gary said I was becoming a couch potato, so he suggested that we ought to be more active when we're together, and games, it seems, are the answer.

We were playing draughts, a couple of rounds before we ate supper, and I was winning. We usually chat during a game, but we don't talk about anything particularly serious, so this evening was exceptional.

'You don't seem to be going out on your bike as much,' Gary said.

I picked up my white draught and hopped over two of his black. I could see he was annoyed.

'You're on good form tonight.'

'Thanks,' I said.

'And the bike?'

'I went out yesterday morning.'

'I thought we agreed that you'd go for a ride every morning.'

I was waiting for him to take his turn.

'Your move,' I said.

'This is more important.'

'I'm not arguing with you, Gary. We're playing a game. That's all.'

He moved a draught forward. I could see he hadn't given it any thought and he'd created a vacant square behind his piece that left it open to be taken. So I did.

'Brilliant! Thanks very much!'

'What do you expect me to do? You weren't thinking.'

'Let's stop.'

'Don't be petulant. Just because you're losing.'

'I'm concerned that you're not taking enough exercise. We've always said that regular runs and bike rides were bound to keep you mobile for longer than not exercising at all.'

I sat back. It was clear he wasn't going to let this one go.

'It's not what they're saying at the care centre,' I explained. 'The neurologist says that too much exertion, if I over-use my muscles, is bad for me.'

'I don't understand the logic of that.'

Rather meanly, Gary spotted a vulnerable white draught of mine and surprised me by taking it. I'm fascinated by the way his mind works. He was reluctant to play when I suggested a game and as soon as it was clear he wasn't winning, he lost what slight interest he might have had, and yet, even in the throes of what was quickly developing into an argument, he couldn't resist taking advantage of my distraction. I had to laugh.

'What's funny?'

'You! I thought you didn't want to play.'

'I don't!'

'Then don't take my pieces!'

He returned my draught to the board and turned away.

'What they say at the care centre,' I said, 'is that tiring the muscles may accelerate their deterioration.'

'But that goes against everything one has ever learnt about good health and muscle wastage.'

'I know. MND is, apparently, different.'

'So what are you going to do? Just give up?'

I thought he looked angry at that moment, as if I had rescinded an agreement, an understanding that we had an approach to my disease that, though not guaranteed to work, made sense to us and, at least, offered some light at the end of a dark tunnel. As I watched him, his anger turned into something deeper. He was upset, betrayed.

'You're not going to fight it?'

'I didn't say that. At all.'

This was the first time we'd discussed exercise. I suppose I hadn't fully come to terms with the fact that, over the last few weeks, I'd abandoned my original plan of a daily swim or cycle for an hour or so before work. It hadn't been a decision as such. I'd had my regular monthly meeting with the neurologist and taken on board his caution about excessive exercise and then I guess I'd just slipped out of the routine, not entirely, but I'd reduced my morning bouts to every other day and, then, again without conscious intention, to one morning in three. To be frank, I'd not thought Gary would notice, but he was evidently observing me more closely than I'd imagined.

'How often *are* you going out?' he asked. 'From what I've seen, it's no more than twice a week.'

'That's about right, Gary. Some weeks it might be three times.'

'And you've stopped going to your club. Who was it you used to cycle with? Sally? Wasn't that her name?'

'I gave that up months ago. I haven't seen Sally for ages.'

He could tell that I was annoyed now. He always thinks that he knows me better than I know myself, and I continue to find that maddening. To that, he's added a level of scrutiny and, I may say, accountability, that I'm beginning to find suffocating.

'I'm sorry,' he said.

'I know. It's okay.'

'I just worry about you. I want you to stay fit as long as you can.'

'So do I, Gary. Believe me.'

'Do you think they're right? At the clinic?'

'Care centre.'

'Oh, alright. Care centre. What does it matter?'

'They've dealt with a lot of cases. I should imagine they know what they're talking about.'

Gary wasn't sure how to react. Part of him, I suspect, clung to the simple notion that, in the face of increasing atrophy, exertion, contraction of the muscles, pushing myself to the limit, must retard the process of the disease, must sustain the life of the tissue that was good. But then he, equally, had to deal with the expert opinion I was receiving. It baffled him, irritated him, aroused fears he hadn't had before, the possibility that advice from the health service might be wrong or misleading.

'Do they– ?' He hesitated. 'Do they tell you what to expect in the future?'

'In broad terms, yes.'

'What does that mean?'

'It means, Gary, that they don't take you through it month

by month. Cases vary. Patients vary.'

'I know, I know. But do you want to tell me what they've said?'

'Not really.'

'Why not?'

If I'd felt the energy to do it, I'd have stood up and walked out on him, but it was quite late, a time when my strength is poor, so I had to content myself with turning away. I spoke with my back to him.

'I have no illusions about what lies ahead. I've had it explained. I've read about it. But that doesn't mean I want to dwell on it. It also doesn't mean I won't fight it. Can you understand?'

'Yes, of course.'

'If we're to get through this together, you have to trust that, at least for now, I am able to make sensible decisions in my own interest.'

'And later?'

That was a question I really hadn't anticipated. How far into the future did he want me to try to look?

'We'll have to cross that bridge when we come to it.'

He didn't like that. I turned back to find he was shaking his head, unsure how he should reply.

'We can't take that approach. It won't work,' he said. 'We have to be honest with one another. You will, who knows when, be unable to speak and, I'm very afraid, think properly, and then it'll be too late.'

'Too late for what?'

'To decide that you've had enough.'

'Enough?'

'You might find you'd rather not go on.'

That shocked me, not because I hadn't had the same thought myself, but because I believed, deep down, that it was *my* thought to have, no one else's, my right, a decision, an attitude – whatever you want to call it – that I should be allowed to consider alone, in privacy. It wasn't, not yet, up for discussion.

I said that I was going to bed.

33

GARY

November 2018

When the day arrived, I was excited, but somewhat nervous. It was partly that I wasn't sure how the islanders viewed what I was doing. I'd enlisted the help of Angus, who closed the post office for the morning, and Fraser, who asked his son to mind the garage while he was away. Angus has, throughout the preparation of the memorial, made no secret of his doubts about it. Fraser hasn't said a word so far, but he has a permanently raised eyebrow whenever the subject comes up, and I know he thinks that I, and the entire project, are barmy, *seòlta*, as Struan Lamont reminded me they say up here when confronted with the unhinged.

Bluntly, I didn't care if they thought that. I had given weeks to painting and varnishing the ladder, and by the time it was finished, I thought it was beautiful. Every evening, I rested it against the wall of the workshop and stood back to appreciate it. It towered over me, a joyful, huge children's toy of a structure, wildly colourful, fit for a giant playroom. Some nights it would make me laugh with pleasure.

You'd adore it, Kim.

With Angus and Fraser, I succeeded in manoeuvring the ladder out of the workshop. We suspended it over the flat bed and cab of the Hilux. I strapped it to the harness rings and wound a rope around it and weighed down the middle with bags of cement. The day was fine and dry, but there was a light wind blowing, so it was wiser to be safe than sorry.

The Hilux had a wide bench seat up front, which took the three of us comfortably. As soon as we set off, Angus was on to me.

'You'll be a celebrity after this, you know, Mr Montrose.'

'That's exactly what I don't want.'

'There's a solution to that, and a three-point turn would serve the purpose.'

'No going back now.'

Fraser said nothing and snorted. He sank down against the passenger door and lit up a cigarette without asking, which annoyed me.

'People will get used to it,' I said.

'Maybe,' Angus said. 'In the long run. But before that, they'll be stopping you in the street, demanding explanations.'

Over the last forty-eight hours, I had worried about this. In the course of painting the rungs and stiles, choosing colours, ordering more paint, sequencing the bands, I'd been too preoccupied with the task in hand to think about any impact my memorial might have. Now, it was obvious. It would be a landmark, probably *the* landmark for the north of the island. It could even become a navigational aid for shipping. That would be curiously satisfying, if it happened. What was certainly true was that people, islanders first but others later, would begin to ask questions. Who put it there? What's it for? I might find myself doorstepped by inquisitive hikers. The question was: would this amount to any more than an occasional inconvenience, an intrusion on my privacy, perhaps once a week, dealt with in five minutes? The question was: would one thing lead to another? Would finding out about the memorial, to whom it was dedicated, what motivated me to create it, spark further curiosity about me and where I'd come from, even about Kim herself?

As we reached the north coast, I drove off the road and took the Hilux up onto the knoll where I intended to erect the ladder. It looked as though we might go about our work undisturbed. A woman was walking her black Labrador on the beach below, tossing a limb of driftwood for the dog to chase. Elsewhere, there was no one around.

We stepped out of the Hilux. The sun had emerged and was bouncing blinding light off the metal work as I began to unfasten the ladder.

'She's running nicely, your vehicle,' Fraser said. 'Been pleased?'

'Very,' I said.

'Should have charged you a few hundred more then, wouldn't you think?'

'I'd have walked away, Fraser.'

'That's what I thought at the time, but that was before I'd heard of your big project. Not so sure now.'

Between us, we lowered the ladder to the grass, and Fraser volunteered to mix the cement. I fetched shovels from behind the seats of the cab, and Angus and I set about digging. The ground was soft from rain, which helped, and we made good progress in the first half hour.

I watched Angus put his back into it and thought how kind these islanders were. I'd offered Angus and Fraser no money. They'd taken time away from their businesses, and the work was hard. They must have felt it was important to support me, to commiserate on my loss in this way. I wondered whether I'd have done the same for them.

We'd dug down three feet or so. I suggested that Angus should take a break. Fraser stepped in to help me and Angus caught his breath while stirring more of the cement.

You'd have been proud of us, Kim, and thankful. Two men you don't know honouring you.

'Goodness! What are you doing?'

She took us by surprise, the woman from the beach. She'd climbed up the dunes and appeared over the lip of the cliff without us being aware of her. Her Labrador danced around the edge of the trench, tempted to jump in.

'Rumour!'

She called the dog to heel and clipped a lead on to his collar.

'Is it to do with some event?' she asked. 'Excuse my nosiness, but it's unusual, isn't it?'

I drove my shovel into the bed of the trench and looked up.

'It's a memorial,' I explained. 'To my wife.'

'Oh, forgive me. You must think I'm very rude. Clara Dunne. I live on the lochan. Over there.'

'Greg Montrose. And I expect you know Angus and Fraser.'

'Of course,' she said. 'For many years.'

Angus stopped turning the cement and stepped forward to shake her hand.

'Lady Dunne is our lord of the manor,' he informed me. 'She owns a good deal of the land up here.'

'Not this patch, though,' Clara Dunne added. 'I'm sorry to hear that you've lost your wife, Mr Montrose.'

'Thank you. Eight months now.'

'Did she have family on the island?'

This was how it was going to be, wasn't it? Not only would the memorial arouse curiosity, but there would be bafflement as well. Why had I erected it here, when my wife died in south-east England?

'No, Kim was a southerner. We did come to the island together, but only once. I live here now, and it felt appropriate. I can't exactly say why. My wife loved the outdoors, the wild.'

'Then it's right and proper. You should do exactly what feels right in the circumstances I always think. Will the ladder simply stand upright out of the hole you're digging?'

'At a slight angle.'

'Marvellous! I'm sure it will look magnificent.'

'Thank you.'

'I'd better leave you to it. Come on, Rumour.'

The Labrador was let off and he leapt ahead, racing along the clifftop, as if he had somewhere to get to in a hurry, a deadline.

Would news of my memorial be all over the island by lunch-time? Clara Dunne seemed like a sensible enough and discreet woman, but how could I tell? She might be an incorrigible gossip.

The foundations were ready, a cylindrical hole four feet across.

'Do you think we have enough cement?' I asked.

'Plenty,' Angus said. 'Have you got those two-by-fours?'

I fetched them from the Hilux, four long, tapered poles that would help secure the ladder while the concrete set hard. We lowered the ladder into the hole, and Angus and I held it up while Fraser shovelled in cement. I resisted a certain sadness I felt at seeing the bands of bright colours, my hard work, sink beneath the grey sludge.

Fraser tipped in the remaining cement, then came to take

my place holding the ladder. I stood back to look at it.

'Bring it down a little,' I said.

I'd settled on what I estimated to be seventy-five degrees to the horizontal, an angle that suggested to me human ascent, not too steep to climb, not too inclined to lose nobility.

'That's it. Can you manage on your own, Fraser?'

He nodded. I handed Angus a length of two-by-four and one of the binding straps I'd brought. We attached each of the timber braces to rungs about a third of the way up the stiles and drove the sharp ends into the soft grass. The other two poles were longer, to prop the ladder higher up.

I went to relieve Fraser.

'What do you think?'

'Terrific,' he said, without much conviction.

The ladder, in my view, sparkled. As I looked up to the top, splinters of light bounced off the rungs and stiles, dazzling me. I had to shade my eyes to see any of it. It was, as Lady Dunne had anticipated, magnificent.

'Bravo, Mr Montrose!' Angus said. He stood well back, admiring.

I'd pictured this moment many times in my imagination, but this exceeded them all. I could not get over a powerful feeling I had of ascending the ladder. I felt I was up there, on the topmost rungs, climbing into the sky, with her, with Kim.

The concrete was hardening. I suggested to Fraser that he could now move away from the ladder.

'We must celebrate!'

There were a couple of wooden pallets on the back of the Hilux, dug out from the workshop, together with a basket of birch logs I'd been feeding the kitchen burner all winter. We dragged them over to the knoll and built a small fire. Angus produced the firelighters I'd asked him to bring, and a bag of kindling, and we lit up. The blaze struggled in the breeze, then took, and I began to smell the wood smoke mingling with salt from the sea.

'We need ourselves a dram, wouldn't you say?'

Angus fetched around in his pockets and pulled out a half bottle of Highland Park.

'Forward thinking,' he said. 'The key to any successful enterprise.'

He handed round plastic glasses and we each took a swig. There was wood smoke in the whisky, soft as it went down. There haven't been many times on the island when I have felt simply happy, perhaps once, aboard Struan Lamont's trawler, but this was another, a deep sense of accomplishment, an odd contentment in friendship, odd because for as much as I felt a bonding, a kindness, between us, Angus and Fraser had no true idea of who I was.

The fire threw flames of light on to the ladder. They glazed each bar of colour. It was as if the memorial had changed its mood. It had been cheerful, exuberant. Now, it was sombre, aware of its purpose, a memento. I felt respectful, uplifted, but aware of my grief.

I miss you, Kim, as always, rapt in you.

'Cheers!'

I had the Highland Park and poured another slug.

'Is that us done?' I asked them.

Their expressions said that it was for me to decide.

'I think so.'

I handed over the whisky and walked to the sea side of the

fire to look back on our work. The ladder rose up above the flames, crane-like, commanding the headland, or so I thought. It was entirely possible that hikers and bikers would pass by and conclude that it was either mad and inexplicable, or the leftover folly of some traditional Viking bacchanalia they knew nothing about. I didn't care. I'd created the memorial for myself, for Kim. If it fulfilled the intention, hikers and bikers could make of it what they wanted.

'Thank you, gentlemen.'

'It's been a pleasure, Mr Montrose,' Angus said.

The flames had died back, and the pallets and birch logs burnt a deep rutilant glow. The heat from them was surprisingly fierce. I felt the burn in my face.

This was it, I thought, the climax to weeks of preparation. The idea of a memorial had come to me quite suddenly, in drink, but for some time I could not imagine the form or scale of it. I looked up at the ladder and felt, again, that it was right. Kim was a woman of hope and a woman in love with colour. She used to quote Ruskin at me, that great travel writer. 'The purest and most thoughtful minds are those which love colours the most.' *Stones of Venice*, I think she said. How true to her! Pure and thoughtful. Even when life spoiled your body and humiliated you, your mind remained generous and sweet. I don't know how you did it, Kim. I really don't.

'Would you join me, gentlemen, in a toast?'

Fraser passed back the bottle and I gave myself a celebratory measure and handed it on.

'To Kim! The most perfect of wives!'

'To Kim!'

'Forgive me all my failings, my darling!'

34

KIM

8th Nov 2017

I have decided to keep writing my diary. I did think about giving it up, when I was first diagnosed, but increasingly I have so little control over my life that I feel a record of my declining health is one way in which I can monitor events and produce my version of what's going on. I don't expect that, as I continue to deteriorate, it will make for very jolly reading, but I want to keep track of what is happening to me.

I have been taking *Riluzole*. The doctor at the care centre, a neurologist called Paddy, put me on it. I say 'put me on', but it was very much my decision. He told me that there was good evidence that certain kinds of MND respond well to it and that it can prolong life by two to four months. Doesn't sound much, does it? But I guess beggars can't be choosers. He said it was up to me, and that not everyone with MND *wants* to prolong life. I decided to go for it.

So far I haven't experienced any ill effects. It will, of course, be impossible to tell whether it's producing any benefit. Life expectancy with this disease is extremely variable, and I could take *Riluzole* for the duration and never know if it had made a scrap of difference. The advice, though, is to start it early, so that's what I've done.

When I was last at the care centre, they took some blood,

'bloods' as they insist on calling the process of draining me into a number of phials. They all came back 'normal'. I didn't ask whether that meant normal in the sense we use the word in the outside world or normal for someone living with motor neurone disease. They probably wouldn't have told me anyway. No, that's unfair. They're good people, and I think they tell me the truth about my condition.

I also had my breathing evaluated. First, they tested what they called my Peak Flow. I had to expel all the air in my lungs, take in a deep breath and then blow violently into a tube. It was a crude little machine. As I exhaled, a tiny metal arrow flew down a calibrated scale. Apparently, it measures how fast you can breathe out.

I then had to go through the same exercise using a Spirometer. A nurse put a clip on my nose, blocking my nostrils. God, that was painful! I took another breath, paused for a few seconds and blew out again as hard as possible into a second tube, this one shaped like a large cigar. The tube was connected to a computer and a screen, which immediately generated figures that meant nothing to me. I was told this test was as much about the amount of air I could hold in my lungs as the speed at which I expelled it. The nurse didn't seem surprised by the results.

I'm sure there's loads more fun of this sort in store for me in months to come.

10th Nov 2017

At present, things are not too bad. I think my conversation is sensible enough. I can wash and dress and feed myself. I continue to work in the shop, though I've reduced my days. Annie has been helpful. She keeps an eye on me and has saved me a couple of times when I thought I might fall. She'll step in with a customer if I appear to be making a mess of it.

Gary has been superb. I can't fault him. He rallies round. He's taken over a good deal of the cleaning and cooking. His fish cakes are especially good. Above all, we're still laughing a lot. God bless him! He makes me laugh every day.

The down side? Well, occasionally, I sense a tingling around my mouth. It's odd, but not unpleasant. I do, though, have an increasing problem with saliva. I dribble a lot and, when I speak, it's often accompanied by a fine spray of spittle. Gary usually laughs and cradles his head. My 'short sharp showers' he calls them.

I find I have to sit a good deal. I have tried to resist it, but I don't have the strength. This is particularly true at work. In the past, I would be on my feet eight or nine hours a day, but I can't manage that now. It doesn't seem to be an issue. I realise that much of what I do with customers I can as easily accomplish while sitting on a chair. It just seems a bit rude, so I usually say something about having weak legs.

With the flower arranging, I find that's not too much of a problem either. I can't stand at the workbench for very long, but if I place a low table in front of me and combine the blooms in a tallish vase, I can manage. Annie often finishes a bouquet for me. I find binding the twine difficult.

I suppose you would say the pace of life is slower. This has its advantages. The other day I was sitting in the shop and the light from the street outside was streaming onto our buckets of flowers. We'd had a delivery a few minutes earlier and the shop was simply full of fresh blooms. They looked so delightful. I could have sat there all day, silently taking in their colours in the autumn sunshine. In fact, I did just that for quite a while. I probably sat there, enjoying the flowers and the light, for upwards of ten minutes.

I am now attending the MND care centre only every now and again. In the first few weeks after my diagnosis, I'd go there practically every day. I wanted as much advice and information as I could get. Now, I go perhaps once or twice a month. They're very good, very supportive. A physiotherapist called James is happy to give me treatments whenever I want. He revives some of the energy I often lack. He manipulates my shoulders, and the muscles in my legs and feet, and my arms and hands. I feel he's improved my circulation recently. My feet don't seem to get so cold.

My inability to stand for long periods is bound to continue and, no doubt, worsen. Atrophy has to start somewhere, James says. No! He's never said that. He wouldn't, would he? But he might as well have done. I look at my legs, the right more feeble than the left, and think – where next? What do I next lose the use of? It's a toss-up what would be worse: my hands, which would mean I couldn't wash or feed myself, or the other leg and losing the ability to walk. Nice!

35

GARY

November 2018

The middle of the day was benign, consolingly warm. I'd driven up to the site on the knoll to check that the memorial hadn't been damaged or even knocked flat in last night's merciless storm. In the early hours, a brutal gust ripped one of the windows in the outhouse off its hinges and left it hanging like a lolling tongue. I had to spend part of the morning fixing new brackets into wet wooden frames. I just hope they hold, but I suspect the whole casement will have to be replaced.

Fortunately, the ladder was unharmed. I was relieved and, in a few short moments, happy. The sky was a riveting blue and cloudless, and I stood under the ladder, the sun's burn on my face.

Do you like it, Kim? Is it as mad as they all think?

Storm or no storm, I'd planned to come up here this morning anyway, to remove the props. I walked around the ladder, enjoying the play of hot sun on the varnished paint. *Purple Pout*, *Sapphire Salute*, *Kiwi Crush*, *Volcanic Red*, those ritzy names. The rungs and stiles gleamed. They flashed flares of silver light, snatched away as quickly as they'd come, thrilling moments that left no trace.

I thought again that it had achieved what I'd intended. As a reporter, travel writer, whatever you want to call me, there are odd moments when I've looked back on what I've written, about Tanzania or Sri Lanka or the Mountains of Morne, and been astonished by how good it is, doubting that I have, in fact, been the writer, had the ability. I felt something similar that morning, admiring that memorial to you, Kim, its beauty, its dignity as it rose up above me, framed in blue.

I moved to the ladder and started to unfasten one of the straps securing the lower prop. As I did so, a gentle wind blew through the rungs, making a song of simple notes and occasional whistles. A line came to me, Britten I think, *Peter Grimes.* 'I hear those voices that will not be drowned.'

This is for you, my darling. I can't tell you exactly what it is or what it means, but from everything I think and feel, I know it is filled with you, your passion.

I turned to the second prop and began to unstrap it and drag it out of the grass.

You permeate it, and it brings you closer to me. I can't explain why, but when I raise my eyes to take it all in, I am as much seeing you, years ago, as this eccentric ladder and its carnival colours.

I shouldered the props and carried them over to the Hilux and threw them on to the flat bed. Then I slammed the tailgate and decided I would take a stroll on the beach before heading home. Descending the knoll, I looked out over the cliff to the pocket-sized island that must be half a mile offshore. It's more of an outcrop of rock than an island, but because of the lighthouse that sits on it, I tend to aggrandise it that way, topographically. An Auckland Westpac had just landed on the helipad and men in orange suits were climbing the metal staircase to the door that would let them into the lighthouse.

Routine maintenance, I guessed, on a rare still morning in the Atlantic Ocean.

The tide was out when I reached the beach. A shallow, Turkish Blue wave rolled slowly up the white sand. Two small children, a boy and a girl, couldn't have been more than seven, were running into the chilly water and running back out again, screaming. I thought of Adrianna, inevitably. She'd have been about five or six, I suppose. I looked around for the children's parents, a guardian, anyone responsible for them, but no one was to be seen. It made me irrationally angry. But they were safe enough, I suspect. I was over-reacting. No doubt there was a parent somewhere nearby, lying out behind the dune perhaps.

I walked on, skirting a narrow band of kelp, a woven thatch of brown leather belts stretching for hundreds of metres along the water's edge. Do they continue to harvest seaweed like this? I've no idea.

There was much to be reassured by on that walk, the kids playing, the shelves of entwined kelp, a landscape largely unchanged in centuries. Will I stay here? It's hard to say. What might compel me to leave? No one from my old life knows I'm here, apart from Sally, of course, but she has no reason to pass on her knowledge. No, I think the decision to go or to stay will be my own, unforced, and that's how it should be.

At present, Kim, my instinct is to remain. This is where I feel, ironical as it might seem, close to you.

36

KIM

6th Dec 2017

I choked on a piece of meat yesterday evening. It was alarming, as much for Gary as for me. He had to watch me struggle. There was no forewarning. Now that Gary has given up his squash, Wednesdays are when we usually have a steak supper. Gary bought a couple of pieces of ribeye, which we had with grilled tomatoes and mushrooms, and those thin fries I like. They're so much crisper than fat chips.

We sat down at 7.30, I think. Gary opened a bottle of Rioja he'd been keeping, and we looked set for a lovely evening together. I'd scarcely begun my meal when a bit of the steak caught in my throat. It wasn't undercooked or especially tough. It just snagged and wouldn't go down. I tried swallowing, gave myself a large gulp of wine. It made no difference.

When I started coughing, I realised I was fighting to breathe.

'Are you alright?' Gary asked, concerned.

'Water!'

He fetched me a glass and I swilled it down, but the choking continued. I could feel the lump of meat in my airway, sat there. It seemed huge, much larger than what I'd put on my fork. My throat muscles were just too weak to move it. I coughed, snatched breath, coughed again.

Gary came around behind me and smacked the middle of

my back. That provoked more coughing. I was gasping now, even thinking 'Is this it? Is this how I go?'

'Cough harder!'

He was shouting.

I did. I drew in as much air as I could and coughed, exaggerating it, retching. The piece of steak eventually came free, shot up into my mouth and I spat it out.

I was so relieved. It had seemed touch-and-go for several minutes. When I was struggling to breathe, I was convinced I'd soon pass out.

Gary held my face in his hands and kissed my lips.

'Thank God!'

'That was horrible,' I said.

'No more Wednesday steak for you.'

'Oh, don't say that, Gary. Not yet.'

'You nearly didn't make it!'

'Nonsense. Look at me. I'm fine.'

It did, however, get me thinking about Christmas, which is fast approaching. Both our parents, Gary's and mine, are dead, have been for years. Gary has a brother, who lives in Wales. They haven't seen each other in a long time and we've never spent Christmas with his family. And I'm an only child. So, we aren't used to family Christmasses. But we do sometimes have friends round. We'd left it very late, but I had been wondering about inviting Annie for Christmas lunch. She's never been to our house, and it might seem strange that it's only occurred to me to ask her now that I'm ill, but she's been very good to me over the last few months. I couldn't have had a more supportive colleague. I don't think the business would have continued without her.

I had also thought I might invite Penny from down the road and her husband. We could even have asked Chloe and Patrick Dobbs for drinks, either mid-morning or early evening, but I don't know that Chloe has ever forgiven me for ruining her carpet last New Year's Eve. We haven't spoken much since.

My choking fit, though, has given me pause for thought. Perhaps we shouldn't entertain people to meals, given that there is a risk the choking could recur. Drinks might be safer. On the other hand, that probably excludes Annie. She lives on the other side of town and it would be a long way to come for a glass of Prosecco, and she'd have to drive, so she couldn't have much.

Oh dear! This requires thought, and less than two weeks to go.

7th Dec 2017

I hadn't intended to write every day, only when things happen that mark the progress of the disease and how I feel about them. Well, it seems that progress – laughable word – can be more rapid than I expected. Yesterday, it was choking. Today, it was a fall on the stairs. Who knows, perhaps this diary will have some value as a record of what people with MND go through.

I fell around 5pm. I was tired, always am by late afternoon. I was coming downstairs and tripped on the last but two and went forward. I could have smashed my face on the hall floor, but instinctively I threw out my hands to save me. I hit the carpet with a hell of a force, unevenly, so that the impact was almost entirely on my left hand. The pain was excruciating. I could hardly call out. I suppose I'd been lying there for two or three minutes before Gary found me. He got in such a state, as ever, fretting around me.

I told him to stop fussing and see if he could get me an immediate appointment with our surgery. I was in so much pain I thought I must have broken my wrist. Fortunately, one of the GPs, someone I didn't know, was prepared to see me, and she confirmed that it wasn't a break, just a sprain.

Just a sprain! I took ibuprofen and paracetamol and it still hurt like the devil.

Gary said my accident was an opportunity to begin a discussion about wheelchairs. I had to laugh. He's nothing if not a forward planner. His view is that we'll soon need two chairs, one for downstairs and another for the bedroom. I'm afraid I teased him. 'And between the two?' That stumped him for a moment. Then he said we could get one of those Stannah stairlifts. He was so funny.

'Are they the only people who make them?' he said, and I replied: 'I've never thought about it, frankly.'

It's kind of him to consider my impending needs. He's much more aware of the help I'll require, all the equipment, than I am. I don't bother about it. Perhaps I should, but it's depressing to think about how incapacitated I'm likely to become. There I go! *Likely.* There is no 'likely' about it. I *will* become incapacitated. Undoubtedly. Definitely. Absolutely. I shall lose all my dexterity, my musculature, my flexibility. This is why I don't think about wheelchairs. The future is bleak. No one is going to heal my broken wings.

11th Dec 2017

I am reading long novels – on my Kindle. My left hand isn't good enough for me to hold up fat books. If I'm not at work, I can sometimes read all day. Long American novels seem to suit my mood. I finished *The Grapes of Wrath* last month and I'm now well into *Moby Dick*, skipping most of the stuff on the anatomies of whales, which I couldn't stomach.

They're both stories about journeys, about movement. I used to love long journeys. With Gary. I suppose it's the hiker in me. And the travel writer in him, of course. I thought I'd chosen these books at random, a quick scan of our bookshelves, but perhaps there were other, latent motives at work, a desire to immerse myself in journeys I can no longer embark on. I don't think I'll ever take a road trip down Route 66 or weather a storm at sea. I might laughably say: those days are gone.

An occupational therapist visited today. Apparently, they hold monthly meetings about me at the GP surgery. They're all there: Dr Bruce, the Practice Nurse, a District Nurse, palliative care people. They discuss my needs and what actions to take, hence the OT. She's going to organise handrails throughout the house.

I've bought Gary a winter jumper for Christmas. Online.

Sometimes I want to scream, but the stress it would cause Gary makes it just not worth it.

37

GARY

18th December 2017

'Could we go out?'

I'm so accustomed to spending our time together in the house that it rarely occurs to me that Kim might like to go on a trip somewhere. When she asked if we could, I felt guilty. Why hadn't I thought of it more often?

'Of course, sweetheart.'

I suspect some of my thoughtlessness has to do with the wheelchair. When you set to it, it's not that difficult to fold up and pack into the boot of the car, but in advance I always expect it will be. We bought a lightweight model, for use downstairs and outdoors. I was surprised by how cheap it was, half price online, under £300. It's aluminium and the foot and armrests adjust easily and it's simple to steer, so that Kim has the freedom to move around independently when she wants to.

She didn't take to it without reluctance. In the early days of the disease, when she fell and we didn't know that it was MND, we'd joke about her needing a wheelchair one day. It seems cruel now.

'You'll never catch me in one of those things!' she'd say. 'I simply won't allow my body to seize up.'

The confidence we had, arrogance even, imagining she could defy the enfeebling power of a disease no one understands or can explain the causes of. Looking back, it's as if we were living in a different century then.

Kim is able to move on her own from the wheelchair to the car, but I have to hold her under her arms for the last part of the manoeuvre, lowering her into the passenger seat.

The chair is fitted with quick-release pins, as are the footrests. They come off in a jiffy, and collapsing the frame down takes no time at all. I should say from the front door to departing is probably no more than ten minutes. There is no real excuse for us not getting out more.

It was a warm day, thin trails of white cloud scattered through a clear sky. I didn't tell Kim where we were going. I thought I'd surprise her. I was aiming for Winchelsea, a place we'd many times intended to visit, but never had.

We drove in silence towards the coast. We do still talk. Considering the limitations, the saliva problem and the diminishing strength of Kim's voice, we talk a striking amount. But I have noticed that there are specific times, perhaps driving in the car, certainly during our evening meal, when we fall silent. It must, to some degree, reflect the long periods we are together in the house. Having done little or nothing earlier in the day, we often lack experiences to draw on, impressions from the outside world. Occasionally, I bring up an item I've seen or heard on the news, or read in a magazine, and that can lead to conversation, but I think Kim is too preoccupied with her physical life most of the time, the minutiae of her decline, to make room for much else. If a news story has implications for years to come, I suspect she feels she cannot afford to care.

I don't often discuss my work. My abiding sense of melancholy isn't helped by re-living the working day at my desk.

Perhaps I'm jaded. The articles I receive by email seem to me dull. There's the odd remarkable piece. As a matter of fact, I received one only the other day. It was about Orinoco crocodiles in Venezuela. But generally, it's the same old stuff. I have been editing travel guides, of very mixed quality, for over fifteen years, I realise. I'd planned to leave with a severance payment, but once Kim fell ill, I began to forget things, lose concentration. The key date slipped by and I missed the deadline to apply for the redundancies that were on offer, and which I unquestionably would have qualified for. Now, when the time comes that Kim's needs and the demands of the job become incompatible, I shall simply have to resign.

One of the oddities of Winchelsea is that although it stands on a hill, it is a cinque port and features the stern of a medieval sailing vessel in the town's coat of arms. The explanation is that, long ago, the town moved from a point on the English Channel below. Sand and gravel, repeatedly deposited on that stretch of coast, eventually choked up the old harbour. Edward the First ordered that a new town should be built on the hill and the maritime activity that had once defined Winchelsea migrated eastwards to Rye.

We lunched at the pub in the town square. I had a BLT. Kim had a tuna sandwich. Tuna is less likely to catch in her throat, so on these infrequent occasions that we do go out, she tends to avoid meat. The girl at the bar asked if she'd like it toasted and for the same reason we said no.

'How many years have we been meaning to come here?' Kim asked.

'Far too many.'

'I can't remember why we wanted to. Had someone

recommended Winchelsea to us?'

'I can't remember.'

'There must have been a reason.'

'Yes, Kim, there must have been, but I can't recall what it was.'

She will insist that there is an answer to every question, if only she pursues it doggedly enough. It can be trying.

We visited the church. When it was first built in the 13th century, St Thomas the Martyr must have been a vast, gothic structure, the size of a cathedral. But as Winchelsea declined, so did the church. More than half of it appeared to have gone. I started to wheel Kim down the pavement to the entrance. I'd only taken her a few metres when she insisted on doing it herself. As long as the surface she's on is flat, she likes to wheel herself, partly to be independent, partly to give her upper body some exercise.

At the porch, there was a deep lip of stone into the church. I gripped the handles of the wheelchair, tilted it backwards and nudged it forward. Even with much of it demolished, the interior took my breath away. All that remained were the chancel and two side aisles, but the avenue of stone columns and the high, vaulted roof were stunning. I could tell from the ruminative way in which Kim wheeled herself up the nave that she, too, was in awe.

'Magnificent!' she said. 'Is there a leaflet?'

There was.

'It seems to have been attacked in almost every century since it was built.'

'Attacked?'

'What's it say here? Raids by the French in the 1300s, church despoiled. Reformation damage. And then Puritans smashed all the windows.'

'How sad. It must have been so, you know, imposing in its day.'

'John Wesley called it a poor skeleton.'

'Better than that now.'

To me, the church smelt of damp and wood polish. Kim said she hadn't noticed. At the altar, she turned her chair to the left and wheeled it towards a series of marble effigies of lords and their ladies, laid out in huge, tented sepulchres the colour of iced tea. She ran her fingers over the polished hands of a knight in prayer.

'They restored the church in the 20th century. All this glass is new. Relatively.'

'It looks it.'

Above us, in the east wall, was a broad expanse of stained glass. Knights and pilgrims were drowning in an azure sea, a soldier-angel perched perilously on a writhing purple demon caught in a breaking wave, pipers and monarchs and disciples all bathed in blue drowning light. Some were martial and triumphant, others obeisant or stern, the Virgin alone, set in white, suckling her stone grey, puzzled child.

Kim swung round and drove herself to a fluted column close to the altar.

'And what's this?'

'Sorry. Can you speak up, my love?'

'I just wanted to know what these markings are.'

The column was scratched and defaced, particularly at Kim's height.

'It's a boat,' she said.

I joined her. Etched into the stonework was a rough sketch of a medieval sailing ship. I could just make out sails and a poop deck. The artist had scored lengths of planking to form a hull and lattices of rigging ran up a central mast. It looked like graffiti, low art, something inappropriate for a church, vandalism almost.

'Why do you think it's here?' Kim asked me.

'I've no idea. Someone snuck in at night and scraped away?'

'Too elaborate. It would have taken hours. Look! There are hints of other ships.'

'Perhaps they weren't all done at the same time.'

We looked again at these curious sailing ships. Their irregular shapes and broken lines, the crude ladders of rigging, reminded me of children's drawings, but the deep scoring of the hulls and masts suggested a powerful hand at work, likely a man with a labourer's muscles. It struck me that he must have been kneeling as he scratched the stonework. Why? It would have been easier to create these images at head height. Their position exaggerated their mystery.

Kim stretched forward and touched the ship's hull with her good hand.

'I think these drawings are so moving, Gary. They're not like those showy tombs over there or the stained glass. They're not done by professionals. I think they were made by ordinary people. So many years ago.'

'Perhaps they were praying.'

'Praying?'

'Well, penitent. It's just occurred to me. You're seeing them from your wheelchair. Whoever did this would have been on his knees.'

Kim turned in her chair. She stretched out and took my hand and squeezed it.

'Do you think it's a shrine?'

'Like flowers left at the spot where there's been a tragedy?'

'Exactly. It's a memorial, Gary. They're remembering an event, people they've lost.'

'Drowned at sea?'

'Maybe.'

We were unexpectedly excited, as though we'd discovered something. I felt that I wanted, needed, to hang on to this moment. Kim might be in a wheelchair, but she was still sensitive and often articulate, able to share in this experience with me, to share her ideas and her enthusiasm.

But as we studied this beautiful rustic tribute, I felt the shadow of sadness was inescapable. I knew then that this empathy, this mutual understanding, would not last long. One day soon she, too, would drown.

38

KIM

19th December 2017

This evening, I fell asleep as soon as I arrived home from work. When I woke up, I could just about remember I'd dreamt about a funfair. Or was it an amusement park? It might have been Disney. The tingling around my mouth was worse and I felt oddly lightheaded, a side effect of *Riluzole*, I'm pretty sure. Perhaps that's why I dreamt.

Gary was squeezing my hand as I came to.

'Are you alright?'

My hand felt small and feeble in his. It seemed to me that he held it tightly and yet it was tender as well. I felt very much loved.

'Yes, fine.'

'You seemed anxious while you were sleeping.'

'I was dreaming.'

Of a ride? Is it called *Star Tours*? We sat in chairs, laid out in rows as they might be in a small cinema. In front of us, an unknown galaxy was projected onto a large screen. As we swept through darkness and stars, our seats lurched, mimicking the twists and turns of flight. It was chilly, the cold of space blown at us through vents in the ceiling.

'I was at Disneyland, sweetheart. We were speeding through the universe. In a spaceship.'

I felt a sharp thrill race through me as we flew. Meteorites hurtled in our direction, cannoning off our hull and throwing us into a steep dive. Our seats leapt up and I thought I might be sick as we seemed to plummet through bottomless space.

'It was amazing.'

'And you're sure you're fine?'

'Absolutely.'

I was still there, lost in infinity, dazed by the clustered light of stars and the immensity of it all.

'Are there any flowers?' I asked him. I don't know why.

Gary didn't seem to hear what I said. He apologised.

'Sorry. It's sometimes difficult to catch. You know.'

I tried to shout, but the noise I made was closer to the earliest recording of a human voice, a strangled sound over a century old.

'Are there any flowers?'

'Possibly. Downstairs, you mean?'

'Are there any still alive?'

'A few, I think.'

'In the red vase?'

'I'll have a look.'

'Do you know, I don't think I smell them like I used to.'

'No?'

'It would be nice to have them up here.'

39

GARY

20th December 2017

I was at work in my bedroom, listening to Sibelius's Violin Concerto and editing on my laptop, a piece from one of our regular contributors on what to do in the event that a crisis, an epidemic, say, or a terrorist attack, occurs in the country you're visiting and the airports shut. It was standard advice, contact the embassy or consulate, inform family, stay inside, consult FCO and airline websites regularly.

At first, I thought it was the sound of her distress, crying. I turned off the music, and then I realised that she was singing. I knew that if she saw me, she'd stop immediately and so I moved as quietly as I could to the top of the stairs. It was just possible to lean over the banister and not be seen.

She'd wheeled her chair to the window overlooking the garden. We only have a small patch and I'm afraid it's become overgrown of late. She must have wanted to enjoy its wildness. It was raining outside, the trees gusting, a beech in particular bowing in front of her.

And there she was, singing. Robert Burns.

My heart's in the Highlands, my heart is not here,
My heart's in the Highlands, a-chasing the deer.

To me, it was beautiful. She couldn't sing, of course. Her diaphragm and the muscles in her larynx are too weak to produce consistently audible speech, let alone something tuneful. But that didn't matter. She was trying, and it was close enough, in my view, to be a recognizable song.

I'm pulled up short by an incident of this sort, the fierce happiness of it. She snatches these fleeting moments from the daily schedule of her misery. She enjoyed our outing to Winchelsea. Yesterday, she awoke from a dream that had transported her through space. Her eyes were bright, as she told me about it, in a way I hadn't seen for months.

She stopped for perhaps a minute or two, gathered her strength, her breath, then started again.

> *Farewell to the mountains, high-cover'd with snow,*
> *Farewell to the straths and green vallies below:*
> *Farewell to the forests and wild-hanging woods...*

Episodes like this make me question what is happening to her and what it is best to do. What, as they say, is the direction of travel? If she is capable of such intervals of happiness, does that make the rest, the diabolical rest, bearable? I don't know. If there is respite, how can we talk about The Swiss Option? We dance around the subject, masking the truth in euphemism, afraid I think to acknowledge that we are speaking of her murder. It's a vile, unvarnished word, but that's what it amounts to.

Yet, there are other days, other stark instances, when she shrinks from view, retreats into her frailty, pale and helpless, silently pleading for release.

Chasing the wild-deer, and following the roe,
My heart's in the Highlands, wherever I go.

Her song ended. She spotted me, above her, and smiled her delinquent smile.

40

KIM

25th December 2017, Christmas Day

Gary cooked our lunch. It was good of him to try a traditional Christmas menu, but in some ways I'd have preferred it if he'd stuck to what he knows, his fish cakes or the baked lamb and tomatoes I enjoy. Instead, he bought a couple of turkey breasts and some oven-ready roast potatoes, and we had them with broccoli and carrots. I made the mistake of asking if there was any bread sauce. There wasn't. As an alternative, we had cranberry jelly. It annoyed him that I'd expected bread sauce. It made him feel he'd let me down. I assured him that wasn't the case, but it's impossible to undo the sense of hurt.

After, we had cheese and biscuits, and mid-afternoon a slice of Christmas cake from M&S. Very good.

We didn't talk much over lunch. The problem I have with excessive saliva doesn't seem to be getting any better and interferes when I want to speak. I'm embarrassed when I dribble and words lose their shape.

It keeps me awake at night, actually. My mouth floods with saliva and I can't swallow it or drain it away by spitting. Sometimes, I feel my mouth is overflowing. Once I begin to think about it, it usually gets worse and then I won't be able to think of anything else. It becomes a complete obsession. I'm constantly wiping my lips – with my right hand, of course. The left is decidedly poor now.

The consequence was that I was up early this morning. I tried not to disturb Gary too much and, aided by the hand-rails, I managed to get downstairs without any mishaps. It's a strange feeling being up before dawn on Christmas Day. You feel very much on your own, when there should be a party. It took me back to childhood, the years before Dad left, and the excitement of finding a full stocking. I'd be unable to wait for the light and would dive in, and within minutes all Santa's gifts were unwrapped, my bedroom floor strewn with festive paper. But there was then a long wait until my parents got up and the best day of the year could begin. The hours were long and a bit lonely, as I recall.

I didn't feel exactly like that this morning. I just had a memory of being seven.

We've organised things so that I can make tea while in my chair. I sat quietly with my mug at the kitchen table and stared out at the dark, thinking. How many mornings like this will I have, mornings when I'm, more or less, competent? Behind that thought, a worry that Gary might not like his jumper, except that I knew he would. He'd been dropping hints since September.

Then my mind drifted to the shop. I've reduced my days again. Gary drove me over there only twice this last week, Tuesday and Friday. The weakness in my left hand continues to bother me when I'm arranging. On the Monday, I told Annie I wouldn't come in because I thought I ought to see the neurologist. She was understanding, as always, but I fear she now expects to have to take charge of the business for most of the weeks ahead. What can I do? I apologised, naturally. I think she accepts that this is how it has to be. I'll suggest we raise her salary when I next see her.

Paddy, the neurologist at the care centre, was sympathetic. At the same time, he offered no hope of improvement. The deterioration in my hand is, apparently, only to be expected.

'Physiotherapy could help,' he told me. 'Are there any other things you'd like to discuss?'

There were quite a few, frankly, but I hesitated to bother him with them. I didn't want to make a fuss, and for all I know the excessive saliva and the occasional twitches I get in my muscles – it could be anywhere in my body – may be temporary and have disappeared in a few weeks.

'Would you recommend physiotherapy?' I asked.

'Was it helpful before? I don't think you've seen James for a while. It's very much up to you.'

As it invariably is! How am I supposed to make a decision? I'm not the professional. I don't know what's best for me, and yet all the medical staff behave as if I do.

'Perhaps I should wait and see what happens in the next few weeks.'

'As you wish. You can always change your mind. He's here Mondays, Wednesdays and Fridays.'

They then decided to test my breathing again with the Spirometer. They say it's to do with managing my 'airway'. God, that clip they attach to your nose is agony. I exhaled into the tube, as fast as I could, and a flurry of numbers skittered on to the screen. No one commented and I was sent home. It was a relief.

Back to Christmas Day. Gary loved his jumper, and I was thrilled with my present: a silver necklace with a black pendant and a pair of matching earrings. Gary helped me put them on. They looked very elegant.

We had a whisky after lunch. Gary had bought quite an expensive eighteen-year-old malt. 'Our present to ourselves,' he said. It went down very well, and I think my saliva problem improved slightly, though I might have been imagining that to persuade myself that a glass of scotch was the ideal remedy. That way ruin lies.

We watched a Bond film, *Live and Let Die*, and then Gary disappeared for a few minutes and came back waving a DVD at me.

'It's a surprise. I had it transferred.'

'What?'

'You'll see! Don't be so impatient!'

He put it on, and suddenly there I was in the Highlands, drenched and laughing. The sound of the rain was fierce, rain falling directly on to the camera mic, rain battering our Gore-Tex jackets. The day was heavy and grey. I was climbing a moor, striding towards the camera in waterproof trousers, and everywhere heather, all a subdued mauve. I looked happy, shouting something to Gary that couldn't be heard through the rain.

'You're telling me you've got bog water in your boots,' Gary explained.

I started to cry. There was nothing I could do about it. The tears were unexpected and overwhelming.

'I'm sorry.'

I tried to pull tissues from my dress pocket with my poor hand, and failed.

'My darling, what's the matter?' He was bringing me tissues. 'I thought it would entertain you.'

'It does. It's just.'

I took a tissue from the box he held out to me and wiped my eyes and blew my nose.

'Sorry.'

'Don't be. There's no need.'

'It's just the contrast.'

'Oh God! How insensitive of me. I didn't think.'

'No, it's fine.'

It wasn't fine really. Seeing those pictures of me full of health, able-bodied, fit, nearly broke my heart. I will never enjoy that strength again, that freedom to do as I like with my body. And would I ever be as happy again? Not like that. Not laughing as icy rain dribbled into my eyes and my feet froze in sodden socks.

The DVD was still playing. I was waving at Gary, inviting him to join me. He started walking in my direction. The picture bounced up and down, but then abruptly settled on my face, smiling. There was light in my eyes, joy. The screen went black.

When we went to bed, we tried to make love. We don't often make the effort these days because it's not easy for me, and can result in pain and frustration. But Christmas night we felt was special, and after the upset of the DVD, I sensed that Gary wanted to show me affection, to be close.

We succeeded, I would say! Not like the old days, but I enjoyed the warmth of his body, and he was careful not to lay his full weight on me. When he climaxed, I nearly cried again. I felt pleased, but I couldn't help feeling that we were snatching a moment of pleasure while we could. I hugged him tight to me with my good arm.

'You're all I've got,' I said.

41

GARY

November 2018

I was down to the boat by seven. Struan Lamont had popped a note through my door to say he was going out in the morning and would I like to come along.

The quay was, as usual, banked up with lobster pots and old nets made of silk thread. There were fewer people on this trip, three of us invited guests, Iain as crew, plus Struan. He leant on the gunwhale and handed me on to the deck.

'My second adventure.'

'Aye,' he said. 'I'm sorry it's been a few weeks, but you'll understand I have to put emphasis where the money is and prioritise my paying clients.'

I couldn't quite tell if this was prickly, a suggestion that I should be paying too. But then why invite me along? He didn't appear put out, gave me one of his gap-toothed smiles, in fact, so I let it go.

Iain appeared from the wheelhouse, dressed in wide-legged yellow waders, a matching jacket and sou'wester. He made the rest of us look dull.

'Will you be having tea, Mr Montrose?'

'I certainly will. Thank you.'

Struan was at the stern, noisily loading beer crates and a sack of potatoes from the quay. I made my way down to him. The water in the harbour was kicking up in the wind, and I held on to the gunwhale and whatever else I could grab, as I felt the boat roll under me.

'It'll be worse out there,' Struan said and he pointed beyond the harbour to a big sea.

'You're happy to go out, then?'

'Ach, yes. The forecast's good. We'll bump around for a bit, but it'll be calm where we fish.'

'If any of us are fit to cast a line by then!'

'Ach now, Mr Montrose, I'll have no Jeremiahs on my boat.'

Kim would have appreciated the sentiment. I was always the one to worry, when she was ill, to fear the worst. She took the opposite view, saw only the possibility of recovery, of winning. I'm glad to say she managed to hold on to that until almost the very end.

I stood outside the wheelhouse and drank a mug of Iain's tea. It was thick and hot. Struan was casting off and Iain gunned the engine and span the wheel. Rackety seagulls swept over us and I felt a chill bite my cheeks as we pulled out of harbour.

'There's good mackerel off the north,' Iain shouted over the wind.

Mackerel! God save us!

'Anything else?' I felt as if I was pleading.

'Saithe possibly. Could be some whiting or haddock.'

He pressed out his roll-up on the wheel bar and took a swig of tea.

'You never know this time of year,' he added.

We were heading in the direction of Kim's memorial. I'd visited it by road, of course, but this would be my first opportunity to see it from the sea. I watched the hard coastline. Dozens of oystercatchers were wading on the foreshore, gannets hovering high. The iron red rocks seemed to shout their hostility to fragile wooden hulls like ours. Grey seals lounged on them, heads dipping and stretching in curiosity as we passed.

The seagulls were still following us, hopeful, bright white. I found the sun blinding. Then a great shelf of sea burst across the bow and drowned the deck. I went sliding in my gripless boots and just about held on. I could see Struan laughing in the stern.

We rounded the headland a little short of nine o'clock, and there it was. Up on the cliff, tall and steeply angled, the ladder stood like a giant salute to Heaven, my *boutade* of colours, as Kim might say, caught in sunlight.

It's yours, my love. In your honour. It does you proud.

'Makes this stretch of coast a sight more attractive, doesn't it?'

Struan was at my elbow. He'd come up to me without my realising and was standing away from the wind, threading bait on to a fish hook.

'It does.'

'Always looked blighted before. Forgotten by God, I used to say. I thank you, Mr Montrose.'

'I think she'd have appreciated it.'

'Your wife?'

'Kim. Yes.'

'Aye, no doubt, no doubt.'

He shouted at Iain in the wheelhouse. I couldn't tell what he said, but evidently this was where we were to anchor and test the waters for fish.

'You'll take this one.'

Struan handed me the rod he'd been baiting and hurried

towards the stern. He threw over coil after coil of chain and the weight of it took the anchor skimming off the deck.

'Full astern!' Struan yelled.

Iain geared down the engine and gradually we slowed and stopped and the three of us who'd come to fish prepared to cast. I hadn't held a fishing rod for a month. I enjoyed the feel of the grip, the weight, the sense of entering on a challenge. I glanced up at the cliff and Kim's ladder.

Wish me luck, my love!

I released the lever and, as I leant back and swung the rod forward, the line spooled out, the hook dived into the water. I sensed the moment of attack, the announcement of sport, swiftly followed by a shy silence, a humbleness. The sea is great. I am a mere fisherman, I thought, entreating its gifts.

'Felt anything?'

Struan again, at my side.

'Not yet.'

'You will. Bound to here.'

He holds a teamug with both hands, appears to have no interest in fishing himself. His eyes are directed towards the cliff.

'Do you visit much?' he asks.

'Visit?'

'The memorial.'

I'm surprised he's interested, though he did once describe the ladder as sublime, I recall, when I asked him if I might use his land.

'Not every day, by any means, maybe once a week.'

'Do you see her?'

I'm unclear whether he means in dreams or memories or

something quite different.

‘When you’re standing right in front of it, that ladder of yours, do you see the wife you loved and lost?’

‘Occasionally.’

‘And what does she look like?’

The boat rolls and he sips his tea, untroubled, as if this were a conversation you might have any day of the week, on a bus or in the pub, Angus’s store.

I have to think for a moment. When I see Kim, in those moments that catch my breath and force me to reach out for something firm, is she well? Is she young and brimming with the energy of cyclists and hikers? Or is she on her deathbed?

‘It depends.’

‘Aye, on your mood, I daresay. I’m the same. Ishbel can be choking with laughter or about to pass.’

He seems insouciant. Is it so long ago? Will I similarly adjust to memory, picture Kim at her best and worst, and not have to cling to the back of a chair, the table in my workshop? I can’t imagine such equanimity.

‘I saw her through, you see.’

His tone is that of a man giving evidence.

‘You said.’

‘To the bitter end.’

‘I know. You said.’

‘Did you?’

The question is direct. It unsettles me. I tighten my hold on the rod and pretend there might be a bite on the line. I lean back, reel in a few feet.

‘You felt something?” Struan asks.

‘I thought so.’

'A twitch? A pull?'

'I thought so. I think I must have been mistaken.'

'Wishful thinking!'

He laughs, places his mug on the deck, empty, between his feet.

'You were saying?'

Was I? I thought I was doing the opposite of saying, avoiding his question, hoping my sleight of hand might spirit it away.

'You were there when Kim died?' he asks.

What is his interest? Why is he prying into my past? The last time we met, he was more reticent, evasive. Now he appears inquisitive, like a grey seal.

'I was.'

I say it cautiously, not sure where it will lead.

'Steady, man!'

Struan grabs me around the waist while the boat rolls. I throw out a hand to the gunwhale, the rod heavy in my left. A breeze, fresh with sea, sweeps across the deck. I feel its sourness on my skin.

'Motor neurone disease you said?'

'She had it for about eighteen months or so, we think.'

'It's difficult to diagnose?'

'Process of elimination. When it can't be anything else, they say it's MND.'

I am out of practice, Kim. How many times did you and I explain it to others, the irresistible sequence of tests and assessments, consultant after consultant, until they arrived at the dreaded conclusion? I once had it off pat. Now, I reach for each word, the apt phrase.

'There's no cure, I believe?'

‘Nothing. They tell you life expectancy, on average, is anything from two to five years from the start. But how do you know when that was?’

By accident, I’ve leant against him, steadying myself against another roll of the trawler.

‘In a case like Kim’s, we’d no idea when it started. Things happened very gradually to begin with.’

There’s nothing on the line. I’ve cast and re-cast for nigh on an hour now, and not a single bite. Struan suggests I try on the other side of the boat. He crosses the deck with me. He says he doesn’t want me slipping over on the wet boards.

‘We talked of this before, Mr Montrose. I think I might have been a wee bit short with you.’

‘Perhaps we misunderstood each other.’

‘I’m not sure it was that. I think I objected to what you were saying.’

I’ve been trying to be conciliatory, anxious that we shouldn’t argue. Struan, though, persists. Has he invited me out today specifically to grill me? Did he plan this? He doesn’t strike me as impulsive, rather a cautious man, I’d say. And yet, there would have been far better opportunities to challenge me on land. The sea constantly interrupts.

‘You have strong religious views. I quite understand.’

‘Aye, I do. But does it rest there, I wonder.’

‘I was overwhelmed. By the sight of her, you know. Seeing her wither away in front of me, and nothing I could do. She lost all her dignity.’

‘There is dignity in suffering.’

‘Not much in her case.’

‘Very hard.’

'It was. She didn't want to carry on like that.'

This, I realise, is the tipping point.

'I couldn't let her,' I add.

The prudent side of me counsels against going further. After all, if I say what's in my head, a full confession, there'll be no turning back. But something urges me on. Is it a kind of rash indifference? Or is it about the truth? Truth with a capital. I am full up with my own deceit, my secrecy. I did what had to be done. It had its own moral imperative. Where is the shame in that?

'It was for the best.'

We continue to tiptoe around. He touches my extended arm, high on the rod.

'The question I have for you is this: is it for you to decide? You, your wife, is it a decision we have the right to make?'

The fishing rod stretched ahead of me. I was glad of the excuse to look out to sea and not face him. I could feel his eyes scrutinising me.

'I know you think not.'

'Aye, that's right. I don't. When we confronted those very moments you speak of, we had only one duty. That was to endure as best we could.'

'You say *we*?'

'Is there a problem with that, Mr Montrose?'

'It's simply that the suffering, your wife's and yours, Kim's and mine, they weren't the same, were they? Those poor women were being tortured, savagely torn apart by disease. Suffering in both mind and body.'

'We were of one view.'

'Were you though? How could you be sure?'

'Absolutely certain, I assure you. We shared a deep faith, you know. It sustained us.'

Do I believe him? Does faith ever provide succour to the very end? Is there not a time, the eleventh hour, the cliff's edge, when it fails? Wouldn't Ishbel Lamont have rather been helped to go then? To have taken The Swiss Option?

'I felt Kim was crying out to me to save her.'

'Did she say so? That's the issue.'

Did she? Can I pinpoint a moment?

'Sometimes. In so many words.'

'That would hardly stand up in a court of law, my friend. Either in this world or at the Day of Judgement.'

'I don't think either would have the right to judge me.'

'Aye, well, there we differ. In my view, we are in God's hands.'

'God's hands made Kim suffer damnation.'

'I think it's best that I leave you now. I don't want us to say things we regret.'

He spun round and started towards the wheelhouse.

'I hope you feel you did the right thing, Mr Montrose. I really do.'

42

KIM

28th December 2017

I found today in the shop - what shall I say? – a challenge. It's a nightmare parking outside, so Gary only had time to help me out of the car and into my wheelchair. Thankfully, Annie was there on the pavement to meet me. I kissed Gary goodbye and Annie wheeled me inside.

I can still stand, just about, but I require the support of a table or a chair nearby and after five minutes or so, I usually have to sit down. Sometimes, I can scarcely make the effort to get up on my feet. I know it's important to keep active and not surrender my muscles to the disease any earlier than I absolutely have to, but the weariness, the enfeebling wave that sweeps through me, can be overpowering.

I enjoyed Annie's company that morning. She understood how to balance her urge to be solicitous and my need to feel that I was useful in the shop. I don't know what customers make of me. Our regular clients now accept that I will often deal with them while seated, and will tend to be slower than usual, having to rely largely on my right hand. We haven't noticed any decline in sales, but there will come a time when I may have to recognize that I am a liability, in danger of driving business away. As it is, I know people are uncomfortable when I occasionally struggle to speak, either because of saliva or because I simply can't remember certain words.

Thursday was like that.

A woman, I suppose in her late fifties and a tad supercilious, wanted a dozen white roses for her daughter, who'd just given birth. I filled out the details of the hospital ward she was on, the time of delivery, the message from mother to daughter. I processed the credit card payment and then I thought I'd make conversation, ask about the baby.

'Is it a boy or a girl?'

'A little girl.'

'Have they given her– ?' And I couldn't think of the word 'name'. It was so peculiar. I knew the idea I wanted to convey, but the word eluded me.

'Have they given her what?' the woman eventually asked. She was annoyed. The conversation embarrassed her.

'I'm sorry. I can't remember the word.'

'Do you mean a name? Have they given her a name?'

'Yes, yes. A name.'

How could I have forgotten it? It was ridiculous.

'No.'

'Oh well, plenty of time.'

'They can't agree on one.'

She laughed, awkwardly, conscious both that she was overheard by Annie and that she had divulged information about her daughter that it was unnecessary to give me. I suspected that if she hadn't already paid for the flowers, she'd have abandoned the purchase and run from the shop. She couldn't finish with me and leave quickly enough.

One day they will find a cure for MND, but too late for me.

Annie assured me there was nothing to worry about.

'Old bag!'

'It was just so strange. Something as simple as 'name'. I couldn't think of it to save my life.'

'We all do it.'

'Really? I know, with more complicated words, sure.'

'No. I forget all sorts of words.'

'You're very kind, Annie.'

'Seriously.'

Except that she wasn't being serious. She was identifying with me to make me feel better about myself, about behaving in a way likely to put off customers, about the imminence of my decline. I was grateful, but not fooled, and if Annie is not going to be the arbiter of my failures, I shall have to be.

I don't give in to bad thoughts much, just on occasion. I can't bear the prospect of losing my mind, failing to remember words and names, all the memories that are so precious to me now. I'm frightened I might just cry and never stop if that were to happen. And yet, when that woman walked out of the shop, clearly exasperated with me, what I felt was humiliation, an appalling realisation that I was an embarrassment to be around.

Too late for me.

43

GARY

November 2018

Later in that same week I'd been out with Struan, I drove over to your memorial. Frankly, I was hoping to be alone with you, my love, but she was there. She had her back to me as I approached and I didn't recognize her at first, not from behind, not even in semi-profile. She was admiring the ladder, touching it, studying the colours of individual rungs.

Then she turned.

'Sally!'

She came over and kissed me on both cheeks.

'Surprised to see me?'

'Well– '

'You know I love this island. I'm so glad Kim recommended it to me. Thought you'd never see me again?'

'It's such a long way….'

'And it's easier to get to Rome or Madrid. I know! It's what people said in the office. But I had a wedding on the mainland, my niece, near Oban, and I thought why not pop across? I like it here. I like the sense of freedom, the wilderness. How are you, Gary? Or should I say Mr Montrose?'

'Fine, thanks. I'm surprised to bump into you *here*. This is the back of beyond.'

She laughed, and returned to where she had been standing,

close to the ladder.

'I ought to say the same about you,' she said. 'What brings you here? And what is this? Is it someone's idea of a colourful joke?'

'All my own work. It's a memorial to Kim.'

'You– !'

'She was all about colour. I wanted to put something on public display that said that.'

'I'm so sorry. I'm always putting my foot in it, aren't I? My big mouth. I should have thought to ask before jumping to bloody silly conclusions. Forgive me.'

'Nothing to forgive. A lot of people think it's strange, and I don't really disagree. It's just what came to mind, and it felt right to me. That's all the explanation I can offer.'

'It's beautiful in its own way. I love the variety of colours. It's like a kaleidoscope. Why didn't you add her name?'

She'd made a good point. Why hadn't I included your name? I suspect there was part of me, this showy memorial notwithstanding, that wanted to keep you to myself. I didn't like the idea of sharing you with others, with islanders. So much of my grief is riddled with inconsistency. How can I make such a public tribute to you and, at the same time, crave privacy?

'Are you here for long?'

'That's kinda up to you,' she answered. 'I was wondering whether I might stay for a few days. I could get a room in the hotel, but if you were willing to put me up, I could stay for longer.'

'Well– '

'Not if it's an inconvenience.'

I felt unsure how to continue. She'd remembered that

awkward moment when Angus had addressed me as 'Mr Montrose'. Was it a good idea to allow her to prolong her stay?

'I realise we hardly know each other,' she said. 'Do say if you'd rather not.'

'No. You'd be welcome.'

Did I mean that? I didn't really feel I had a choice. It would appear discourteous to have said no, and I wouldn't want her gossiping at the hotel. *Of course, he hasn't always gone by that name.* It would be all too tempting to brag, arouse curiosity.

Is this paranoia? Am I losing my way, going crazy, imagining risks and threats that don't exist? I considered whether I should stipulate a number of days, but again, it would inevitably come across as rude.

'Stay as long as you want.'

'That's very kind, Gary. I have to be back at work at the beginning of the month, but it's good to know there's an open invitation.'

Is that what I'd said, what I'd implied? I hadn't intended to. Good God, I scarcely know her. She said as much herself. And what do I do about the problem of names? *Montrose* was one issue, but I was also going to have to point out that I wasn't known as Gary on the island. What possible excuse could I find to explain that? If it wasn't so incriminating, it would be comic.

'Do you think you're here for the duration?' she asked.

'I haven't made up my mind.'

'I don't suppose you'd have built this memorial if it wasn't a serious possibility.'

'No, that's true.'

'Don't you find it lonely?'

She smiled at me in a way I found hard to read.

'Not particularly.'

How had she got here? There was no sign of any other vehicle.

'Can I take you back to the village?' I asked.

She laughed.

'No, no, I've got a bike.'

'Where is it?'

'It's down on the beach. I climbed up.'

'We could throw it in the back of the truck. It's quite a way to the village.'

'No, I'd much rather cycle, Gary. It's a beautiful day. I'll enjoy the ride.'

'Okay. So, when shall I see you?'

'Around teatime? Is that alright with you?'

Teatime. How quaint! Perhaps she thought people on the island hadn't changed with the times, were stuck in the 1950s, enjoying their teatime with scones and jam and buttered teacakes and iced buns. Not at all what was on offer at my place. I might have some shortbread, maybe a few digestive biscuits, bound to be stale.

I started up the Hilux. Sally was making her way to the clifftop. I watched her climb over the low stone wall that ran along the line of the cliff. She was athletic looking for her age, I thought, just as Kim had once been.

The sun fell directly on my windscreen as I drove back. Turning corners in the lane, it blinded me and I slowed down to avoid erring into the hedgerow. I was thinking about Sally and what was in store for me over the next few days. There were times when I was lonely, I had to admit. I'd been lying when I told her I didn't mind the solitude. It might be entertaining to have her around for a while. There would be potentially difficult conversations about Kim, of course, but we needn't discuss her the whole time. We'd find other things to chat about. We might even have the occasional laugh.

44

KIM

31st December 2017, New Year's Eve

It seems hardly credible that it was a year ago that we went to the Dobbs' New Year's party and I spilt that glass of wine and collapsed on the carpet. I still feel embarrassed thinking about it, even though it wasn't my fault. We've not seen Chloe and Patrick since, and there was no invitation to their party this year. Not surprising, I suppose. They must have heard what has happened to me, but I expect they think I disgraced myself all the same. I imagine everyone did. Apart from Gary, Sally was the only sympathetic person in the room. And I did ruin Chloe's carpet.

I went to the care centre on Friday morning. Gary drove me, and then he went on into town. He was after some book. I can't remember the title.

Unusually, Paddy, the neurologist couldn't see me immediately and I had to wait in the lounge. It was, frankly, depressing. I know I've been very inward in the way I have approached this disease. I have given thought to the impact on Gary, but for the most part, I've only considered how it might be affecting me, what I can and cannot do, how it is progressing and how I feel about that. But waiting in the lounge, anchored in my wheelchair, I couldn't avoid my fellow sufferers.

It terrified me. So many of them were far worse than I am.

I spotted one man in the corner, who seemed to be entirely alone and uncared for. His arms hung loosely on either side of his wheelchair, and he couldn't hold his head up. I could see he was trying. He would lift his head for a few seconds and then I guess the muscles in his neck weren't strong enough and gave out, and his head fell forward. He was smartly dressed – blue check shirt and a plain, red tie that might have been a Christmas present. Perhaps someone *was* caring for him. He'd lost control of his legs, which twitched every now and then. He caught my eye. I think he was embarrassed to be noticed, but he tried to smile and, as he widened his mouth, a dribble of saliva ran down his chin on to his tie.

I very nearly cried.

'That's Sam,' my nurse explained, my regular nurse, Barbara, Barbie we call her. 'He's brave, our Sam. He can't talk any more so there's no chat with the others. But he likes to be in company, especially at Christmas time.'

She'd come to tell me that Paddy was ready to see me. I was grateful to get away from the lounge. I'd begun to feel I was looking into the future, and there wasn't much to be cheerful about.

The appointment was brief. I like Paddy. He's kind and good with me, unlike the other neurologist I occasionally have. I always come away satisfied that I've understood what Paddy had to say and what I must do. But he's never given me any grounds for optimism. He's never suggested this symptom or that is just a passing phase and will eventually disappear. On the contrary, everything I complain about is, in his experience, typical and to be endured.

This morning I wanted to talk to him about my deteriorating voice.

'I'm so quiet,' I said. 'My husband says there are times when he can't hear a word I'm saying. He asks me to repeat what I've said quite a lot.'

Paddy appeared surprised.

'It can be a problem,' he said. 'I can't say I'd noticed it in your case.'

Was that encouraging? Was he familiar enough with my voice to detect a difference? I wanted to take comfort in his opinion, but Gary has known me for over twenty years. When he asks me to say something twice, it isn't because he hasn't tried to hear. He knows there's a developing problem, and I can tell that he strains to pick up every word. If he can't make out what I've said, I reckon no one can.

'Perhaps you need to make a greater effort to raise your voice.'

'I do.'

'Are you making an effort now?'

'Yes.'

'And I can hear you perfectly. What about at your work? You're still working, aren't you?'

'Sort of. Annie doesn't seem to have a problem. At least, she hasn't said so.'

'There is a speech therapist here at the clinic,' Paddy said. 'I could put you down for a course of treatment. She can come to your home, if you like. Have a think.'

'I will. Thank you.'

'And you might like to consider registering for voice banking.'

I must have looked as if I hadn't understood.

'They record your voice, and they can turn it into a programme that allows you to generate speech through a computer.'

He extended his hand and took my good arm and squeezed it.

'You're worrying before you have to, Kim. Just try to be a little more conscious of needing to try when you're at home. You're so used to life with your husband, it doesn't occur to you to speak up.'

'You're probably right. Mustn't fuss about things, must I?'

That was it, the end of the appointment. I was about to mention my saliva problem and thought better of it. He wouldn't have anything to add to what he'd said last time.

Gary was already outside as I was wheeled through the main entrance.

Another year gone, a brand new year about to start. What does it hold for me, for us? It's easy to be gloomy, especially after sitting in that lounge and watching poor Sam. But there are many respects in which I'm thankful. I can still stand for short periods. I still feed myself. I can still talk and, perhaps above all, laugh. We do laugh, Gary and I. God bless him!

45

GARY

November 2018

Sally, it appears, disapproves of drinking during the day. She disapproves, to be exact, of my drinking, particularly at this time in the afternoon, 'teatime' as she puts it. It was about five, and she'd turned up prompt to the hour. I heard the clatter of her bike as it fell against the wall. Then she was at the kitchen window, a suggestion of redness in her cheeks, a broad smile. She could see me across the room, settled at the table, whisky in hand. But still she knocked on the glass.

'I had such a good ride,' she said, vigorously roughing the doormat with her boots. 'When it's fine, the weather I mean, it's glorious up here.'

Up here, as if we on the island live on a raised plateau, above the world, above the cloud line, rarefied.

I make her tea. Perhaps, in politeness, I should have at least offered her a glass of the whisky, but instinctively I knew she'd refuse. Instead, I tug two malted milk biscuits out of the end of a packet and present them to her on a plate.

Now we are sitting together, we struggle for conversation. I search my thoughts for a topic, an anecdote, anything that will fill the silence and avoid memories of Kim.

Her eyes follow my hand as I lift the glass and sip my drink. I relish the taste, even as I see her lips shaping up to admonish me. 'Should you be.....' But she doesn't, checked perhaps by the slightness of our friendship, her dependency on my hospitality.

Late afternoon sun slices across the kitchen, bathes her, blinds me. She has been here an hour and proposes to stay for several days. When we met at the memorial, it seemed like a good idea to invite her. I thought it might be safer than to let her chinwag at the hotel bar, and I'd actually thought it might even be entertaining. Now, I'm less sure. Indoors, mulling over my whisky, I wonder what has brought her to the island. Is it innocent holiday or something more inquisitive?

I am increasingly aware that my world is shrinking. For weeks, I've been distant from the life I once led, its accountability to others, to bureaucracies. But this morning, I received a letter from DVLA, warning me about the absence of road tax for the Hilux. Once I'd paid Fraser the cash, he would have had to pass on my name and address as the registered owner. It appears that if I don't deal with this immediately, I'll face a heavy fine and points on my licence. The tax is simple enough to pay, however odd they might find it at DVLA to receive an envelope of cash. But I suspect insuring myself as Greg Montrose will be impossible.

'I was intrigued,' Sally says, 'last time I was here– '

By what?

'I think it came up when your friend, Angus was it, dropped by.'

'He's not really a friend. I've got to know him because he runs the stores and delivers the post.'

'Of course. I called in there on my way up. He's a bit of a grumpy sort.'

'I wouldn't say so.'

'He was to me. I brought you some fruit.'

'That's very kind.'

'Grapes.'

'Lovely.'

'And apples.'

What intrigues her? I've tried to design a life for myself here that is plausible, without anomaly or irony. But that only succeeds for as long as the witnesses to it are new, have no shared history with me. Sally, in however limited a way, knows me. She can make comparisons.

'I suppose I was surprised you'd changed your name. That's what intrigued me.'

This deserves more whisky.

'Not that you're not perfectly entitled to do it. I knew someone who changed back to her maiden name after fourteen bloody years of widowhood. Can you believe it! Why leave it that long?'

'I wanted a fresh start.'

'Not that you have a maiden name, of course. Not really the same thing, is it?'

Her eyes once again follow the journey of my glass. Does she remember that New Year's Eve, the party at the Dobbs' house, when Kim spilt red wine on their pale green carpet, the inkling of something wrong, the dark stain I was sure I would scrub clean if I were only determined enough, if I resolved to wipe away the evidence?

'Why did you?' she persists.

'As I say, I wanted a fresh start.'

Sally smiles. Perhaps she thinks I'm lying or, more likely, she doesn't believe it's the whole or most important reason. Perhaps it's no more than curiosity. I mustn't allow my mind to run away with imagined possibilities. I have no accurate sense of how well she knew Kim, how good the friendship was. Were they confidantes? Does she know more about me, us, than I imagine?

She places the teamug she's been nursing on the table and steps across the room.

'Come on,' she says. 'There must be more to it than that.'

A better story? This is the first time my made-up account of myself has been challenged.

She hovers.

'When Kim died– '

At first, for three or four weeks, when I thought I had to continue to live in the house for form's sake, I found the associations too near and I struggled. After the toll of care and confinement, I wanted to breathe again. But I had to stay, at least for a while.

I could tell her none of this.

'I thought I might escape here, start a new life, life without Kim, on my terms. I wanted to remember her when I chose to, not because the clothes and the smells, and the furniture, and the photographs on the walls, all those uncalled-for memories, were forcing me to.'

Sally looks considerate, as if she expects to cry.

'It was hard.'

'Hard, yes, but more than that, I couldn't bear the house.'

'No. I understand.'

'Most people, when they're bereaved, want to hang on to all that remains of the person they've lost. But my grief wasn't like that. I wanted fresh air.'

She fears that is all I have to say.

'And your change of name?'

'It was silly, I suppose. More trouble than it was worth. I didn't want to be accountable. I didn't want to have to talk about my past, and I thought if no one could trace me, no one could find out what my life had been like and where I'd come from, they'd stop asking questions.'

'And have they?'

'Kind of. I think I've been accepted here, at least as a visitor.'

Sally walks over to the kettle, doesn't ask my permission, runs tapwater into it, plugs it in.

'Tea?'

Have I convinced her? She is difficult to gauge. At times, she makes mistakes, expresses a thought or an idea that suggests extraordinarily poor judgement of the moment, putting her foot in it, as she says. At others, I suspect discernment. I sense she's weighed what she's heard and, from experience, found it wanting.

What I have to consider is how much of a risk, if any, Sally poses. How persuasive could she be? If she spoke to Angus or Fraser or Struan Lamont, what could she say? That the man who is renting the cottage up on the hill is not who he pretends to be. It's not a crime, after all. Would they care? They might look at me with a new suspicion, but it's not as if they've accepted me as a long-term resident anyway. To them, I'm not an islander. I'm a visitor, a blow-in, bound to leave at some point, memorial notwithstanding.

'We should go walking or cycling together,' she says.

A change of tack? Is it genuine or calculated?

'I don't have a bike.'

'I'm sure we could find you one. We could ride out on the coastal path.'

'We could hire a dog.'

'Hire a dog?'

'Just my joke. I don't think there are dogs for hire.'

'You have a strange sense of humour, Gary.'

46

KIM

6th January 2018

I fear this is my last day in the shop.

After the New Year's Day bank holiday, we took an extra twenty-four hours and re-opened for the start of the year on the 3rd. But I didn't feel up to it. I wasn't there to welcome the old familiars. I was simply too shattered to go in, exhausted, ironical as it might seem, by the Christmas break. It's not that we'd done much, but I found the expectations of my happiness, given my condition, draining.

I came in today because I didn't think I could leave it any longer before at least trying to work, and Saturdays are usually busy. Gary drove me, and I was actually feeling quite cheerful as he unfolded my chair and helped me into it. He pushed me up the ramp into the shop and there was Annie, a bright smile to greet me, bright red nails and heels, Happy New Year and all that, and I still have enough strength in my right hand to raise it and shake a salute. She came over to kiss me. I felt my cheek twitch as her lips brushed my skin. There was nothing I could do to control it. I hope she didn't think her affection wasn't welcome.

As I say, to begin with, I was cheerful and confident, glad to be back in harness. Annie had already sorted out the morning's delivery into buckets, and the January sunlight was blazing through the street windows. The first stems of lisianthus, in their cardinal purple and their pinks and whites, were lit up in a way that made my poor, tired heart lift with gratitude. There is much to be thankful for.

But then Gary left, and my mood changed. We'd been together all through Christmas and there hadn't been a waking hour when I'd not been near him, when I couldn't call on him to help me, if I needed the toilet or had the urge to talk. So, once he'd gone, I felt frightened and alone. Who'd catch me if I fell? Who'd hug me when I felt so weak I wanted to weep and die?

'Shall I fetch us a couple of cappuccinos?' Annie asks. She is half-way through the door to the street.

'No, don't go!'

My voice is scarcely audible, but she understands the urgency. I start to cough and can't stop for several long seconds. Annie closes the door and comes back and holds my left hand and squeezes it. There's nothing left in it. It's just pulp now.

'I'll make us something here instead.'

She means well, Annie. She's been a wonderful support, but she can't have the intuitions that Gary has, his sensitivity to every nuanced change that flutters through my mind and body, like a butterfly on a patch of yellow daffs.

What is to become of me? How long have I got left? It fills me with panic sometimes, thinking about it. I try not to ask the question, as a rule. There is no reliable answer and, in any case, life is better lived in ignorance of it, I believe.

I make every effort to work, creating new arrangements. Annie brings me individual flowers, in twos and threes, and I trim the peduncles and try to balance and contrast the colours and shapes as best I can. But I am nigh on useless. With one hand, and that deteriorating, it's impossible to control both the bucket and the flowers, and I'm constantly dropping stems on the floor. Annie is very good and, each time, hurries over and picks them up for me.

It is becoming evident that she would prefer to work on her own. At one point, I knock a bucket over and let out what seems, for me, a loud 'Fuck!'. There are customers in the shop and Annie, patient as she is, can't help but glare at me. I'm a liability.

I'd hoped I would choose the day when I decided that the shop was becoming too much for me and, with some if not much grace, retire. But this doesn't feel like a choice, far from it. I look at Annie, and she's not much younger than I am, but she has a fit, functioning, attractive body. She moves with ease around the shop floor. When she speaks to people, her speech is clear and intelligible. She's never asked to repeat what she's said. Annie's customers nod and smile and buy their flowers without difficulty or confusion.

And then I see me! I catch something of my body in the mirror behind the workbench. Today, there are vases on the bench, a Sellotape dispenser, rolls of cellophane. They obscure parts of me, but I can see enough of my head and shoulders to be appalled. I don't generally look at myself in mirrors these days. There are never any pleasant surprises and it depresses me. This time, though, I hardly recognize the woman sitting over there. Her head hangs forward, as if she struggles to hold it up. Her hair needs washing. The brightness I remember in the eyes has gone. She appears both grumpy and resigned. Or do I mean forlorn?

I turn away, and Annie says:

'You're daydreaming.'

'Caught me at it!'

It's hardly daydreaming, though, staring at myself in this cruel mirror, certifying the disability I now am. Why has this happened to me? Why me?

'Would you manage - your own, Annie?'

She's surprised. It appears that although she's run the shop very successfully on many occasions, she's always thought of them as temporary, *ad hoc* assistance.

'Why do you ask?'

'Isn't - obvious?'

Is she affecting ignorance of where I'm taking this? All morning I've been illustrating how futile it is for me to be here. I hope she's not going to pretend that everything's fine and I'm making a valuable contribution. Please don't, Annie! Don't patronise me in that way. I'm owed better.

'You think you can't carry on,' she says.

'Obsly.'

'Sorry?'

I take my time, speak methodically. This is important.

'Obviously. Look at me, Annie. This hand's died. My right can do a bit, but I'm forever dropping stuff, breaking things. The customers look at me as though I'm some kind of monster.'

'No, they don't!'

I'm clumsy in a neat world.

'I don't mind, Kim. You know that. I don't mind picking things up. I really don't. I'm happy to help.'

'Not the point.'

It never was the point. I'm not here for charity. Either I pull my weight as a worker or I'm out. I suppose I was only waiting for this moment to arise, now clear as a highland burn.

I'll be sorry to say goodbye to the shop. I built up the business from nothing, from an idea Gary and I had one evening in the pub. I wrote it down on a yellow beer mat so I wouldn't forget. In the early days, before Annie, I used to sit on a stool next to the workbench, wondering when the door from the high street would open. Would I ever see my first customer? The flowers stood in their buckets and bouquets, waiting to wither.

Then, suddenly it seemed, they came in a flood. The phone started to ring. I had four people in the shop, all at once, all expecting to be served, and I had no assistant at that time, no Annie.

The business never looked back. The customers just kept coming. Weddings. Funerals. Birthdays. Valentine's Day. I began to supply hospitals and care homes. There were corporate clients, once-a-weekers, contracts that were the bread and butter I needed between anniversaries.

The whole time, visions of colour. Whose working life is like that? Every day, hundreds of glorious blooms arrived in vans, filling the shop, everywhere I looked, and for the most part, people left a degree happier than when they stepped in from the street. That was my real reward, cheering people up with dazzling colours. You could see it in their faces.

I shall miss it. Them.

47

GARY

November 2018

The air is seasoned with moisture. As we ride, I feel hints of wet scattered in the wind, dampening my forehead and cheeks and eyes, my hands on the bars. But there is not, as yet, rain.

Sally had been determined. I'd tried to put her off to another day, but she has a will of iron, and having borrowed Fraser's mountain bike, it was difficult to come up with any more excuses.

'Today's just right, almost bloody perfect.'

She says it with an insouciance, but at the same time I know that this apparent breeziness dismisses all other opinions. She expects agreement. She expects me to leap over to the kitchen door, whip my coat off the hook, joyous. She reminds me of Kim in this respect.

Her stay has been unproblematic so far. She's slept in the bedroom above the kitchen. It's a shrunken kind of room, narrow and poorly lit, but she has yet to complain. As a matter of fact, quite the opposite, she's been unfailingly cheerful. I've offered to cook her a meal a couple of times, but generally she keeps herself to herself. She's out walking or cycling most of the day, probably takes lunch in a pub, and in the evenings she likes to listen to audiobooks on stringy headphones. She's biding her time, I'm guessing, allowing her presence to sink in.

We drove up the spine of the island. I was convinced that by the time we'd reached the coast, the rain would have swept in. I don't know that Sally would have cared, but in any case it held off. We left the road and pushed the bikes down a gravel slope to the coastal path and the cycle track.

'I told you it'd be fine!'

We are walking now, up a steep ridge overlooking the northern shoreline. The sea is dove grey, blanched by soft light, a fur of spray lifted by the wind from the crest of each breaking wave. I feel slightly cold.

As the ridge flattens out, the cycle track widens and we are able to remount and ride alongside each other. Sally stretches out her hand and clutches my arm.

'Glad you agreed to come?'

There is something weird about this morning and this ride. I suppose it's a sense of déjà vu, a memory of cycling like this with Kim. For Sally to accompany me seems an impertinence, a two-fingered jeer at my marriage, my lost wife. But that's unfair. Sally intends no rudeness, no disrespect. If anything, I think she hopes to jolly me out of my grief, or at least to distract me from it, inject a little levity into my dull life.

She smiles as her hand slips down my arm and encloses my fingers, so briefly I scarcely register it. Is it meant to be reassuring? It's miscalculated, then. It suggests to me an entitlement she doesn't have. I push down and pull ahead of her.

'Isn't this the way to Kim's memorial?'

It hasn't occurred to me. I've always approached it from the other direction and parked the Hilux quite close by. But she's right. This cycle path leads directly to it, about a mile off.

'Have you had many comments?'

She's calling out, and it's a struggle to hear what she says. I'm forced to drop back and ride alongside her again.

'I'd have expected it to be the talk of the village,' she says.

'No, not so much actually. Rather less than I was anticipating.'

'Surprising.'

What is it that annoys me about this chatter? Is it that it's so inconsequential? Is it anything indeed to do with what's being said? Or is it that I am anxious about this woman? Anxious in all sorts of ways. I don't know how to read her gestures. Are they hints of intimacy? There seems to be an assumption of longstanding friendship, but that's nonsense. We barely know each other. What does she want from me?

We have climbed up and now have a broad view across the north of the island. To our right, looking east, a grey sea pounds the harsh, rubiginous rocks that flank the shallow bay beneath us. On the other side, I can see Kim's memorial towering over us, a few hundred metres away.

The ladder doesn't appear to be right. There's something wrong with it. Is it the angle? Has it been damaged? I can't quite make it out at this distance.

'Shall we?' Sally suggests.

We mount up and ascend the hill. I'm pressing on, riding fast.

'You're in a hurry!' she shouts. 'Wait for me!'

But I won't wait for her. Something has happened to the memorial and I want to find out what it is.

As we approach the ladder, Sally is calling out again.

'Is that graffiti? Someone's written something.'

I pull up in front of it. My anxiety that the ladder might

have been damaged, that someone might have tried to knock it down, vandalise it, was exaggerated. But there is graffiti, yes, five words spelt out in capitals in white paint, one word to each of five consecutive rungs, a message.

WE KNOW WHAT YOU DID

'Golly!' Sally says.

48

KIM

15th January 2018

Sometimes I realise I don't give Gary a second thought. He's given up so much for me, his squash matches, seeing his friends at the pub, much of his work. He does all the cooking, the cleaning, washing, shopping. He never complains. I just assume he'll be around to care for me and to raise me up when I feel as if I'm falling down a deep well. Yesterday, after we'd had our evening meal, I looked at him across the dining table. My thought had been to thank him for our supper and to say how much I appreciate what he does for me. But it was like I hadn't seen him in months, not properly. Before I said anything, it struck me with the force of a hammer blow that he was utterly exhausted. He had dark rings under his eyes. He started to clear up the plates and it was obvious from his movements that he scarcely had the energy to do it. I didn't know how to react. I was about to say that I realised how demanding it was to be a full-time carer when he smiled, picked up the tray and left.

The moment was gone. The opportunity to let him know how much I value him had simply slipped out of the room with the dishes.

I wished I could say that one day this will all be over. Of course, in one sense, it will be. I'm on a one-way street and judging by the speed at which I am declining now, the end surely can't be that far in the future. I suppose what I mean is that if the situation were not as it sadly is, if Gary had a goal, the knowledge that he must care for me for, say, six months and then I'll recover, it would make a colossal difference to his mood and expectations, perhaps to his energy levels too. But that can't be, so there are no consolations for him, merely more of the same and, likely, worse.

I fear that's why he drinks more than he should.

God, I write so slowly. Such a scrawl. I did attempt to do this on my laptop, but the loss of my left hand made typing even more laboured.

I imagine I carry out an audit of my physical condition a dozen times a day. It's obsessive, irresistible, like a tick or a spot. By contrast, I try not to dwell on my state of mind. It's not really in my character. I think, if I examine my *feelings* too much, I'm making a fuss. I was brought up to believe that the only proper response to adversity or challenge, is to persevere, to get on with the job in hand, above all to keep quiet about it. But there are some tall mountains that are just too hard to climb, and I'm half-way up one of them.

I had such a shock clocking my image in that mirror in the shop. It was partly that I didn't recognize the woman I saw. I don't see myself as someone slumped and beaten. More than that, I was so distressed to realise how far I've come, how far I've gone. I monitor developments, for sure, but I clearly don't *see* enough. All that I've been aware of lately is that I'm a bit breathless, lying in bed at night. But that day at work taught me that there have been other big changes that have, I think, not registered. It makes me laugh, squirm even, to think that I want to donate my organs to medical research. Who on earth would want them? They'll unpack my body and shrink from the sight of my withered bits and pieces of biology, my wasted life.

I've realised that I'm not as strong emotionally as I used to be. I'm frightened now, of what lies ahead, of the brief time still available to me. The sand has almost filled the bottom of the hourglass. What will it be like, that final moment? I think I'm ready and then I catch myself feeling a kind of terror, coursing through me. I have no control over it. I try to be patient, knowing it will pass, but there are times when that's impossible.

Is it bearable, all this? I know Gary loves me. He demonstrates it every minute of every hour. Would he be better off without me? When the credit and debit account is drawn up, am I too much of a burden? At supper last night, I thought so. A man shouldn't look that done in at the end of the day, nothing left in the battery. We've had a good life together, a happy life, but this isn't fair.

On either of us.

Sometimes, and I don't like to admit this, I go to sleep hoping I won't wake up. The following morning comes and I wish it hadn't. Is that bad of me? I can't tell Gary about it. It would make all his efforts seem futile, hurl all his hopes down that deep well.

And yet, and yet, perhaps that's exactly what he wants me to say? Are we denying ourselves the one sensible solution to this misery? I may be frightened by how little time I have left before my life ends, but am I not frightened still more, petrified, by what must happen between now and then? At the moment, I am standing on the cliff edge, scarcely balanced, teetering, but I haven't begun to fall, to fly down to the rocks, helpless, out of control.

I can still make a decision either way. I want to force my mind to reach a conclusion, to make a choice, to stop the weighing-up, the reasoning, the acknowledgement of the various arguments for and against.

I want to say to myself: *Go for it, Kim, take the plunge!*

49

GARY

19th January 2018

We moved Kim's bed downstairs yesterday evening. I say 'we'. It was, of course, my job alone. It's something we've been putting off for weeks. We took the view that for as long as I could help her go up and down the stairs, it lent a degree of normality to her daily routine. She would come down for breakfast, spend the day largely in the sitting room and return to her bedroom to sleep. It's some months since we shared a room, but Kim nonetheless liked the idea of going *up to bed.*

That's no longer possible. As she has lost motor power, her limbs have become heavier, dead weight, and I can't lift her in the way I used to. The stairs are steep and, up until recently, she'd help me by pulling on the handrail with each step we ascended. That took some of the load off me, if only for a few seconds. Somehow, we'd struggle up to the landing and, once we were on the level, it was comparatively easy for me to help her into her chair and wheel her to her room. If I was in high spirits – less and less these days – I'd throw her over my back. It reminded us of our honeymoon on the island of Corsica.

I could have bought a Stannah stairlift, but we failed to discuss it and somehow the idea just slipped away.

We're fortunate in having a second shower on the ground floor. We put it in years ago, when we extended the kitchen. It filled a gap in the architect's plan. The occupational therapist has had fixed seats built into both showers, so that Kim can sit while I wash her. Frankly, up until now, we've rarely used the one downstairs, but now it's a thank-god. Kim doesn't enjoy showers very much, which means that there's a trade-off between hygiene and comfort. I try to wash her, all over, perhaps three mornings a week, but frequently it's twice, and she generally protests about those.

It's hard to watch her at the best of times. When she showers, her head falls forward, except when she makes a special effort to raise it and then she finds the falling water painful. *Spiky*, she calls it. I suppose it's because her skin is sensitive. It looks the opposite. It's loose and hangs from her neck, her upper arms, her thighs. Her muscles have lost most of their tone. Her breasts are flaccid. She knows this, and she's embarrassed, another reason why she's reluctant to shower. We remember what we call The Days of Health, when her body aroused me. She knows that when she's naked now, I view her with pity and sadness, and that in those moments love somehow isn't quite enough. It's all there is, though, stolid and reliable Love, and it gets us through most days. It's just that it doesn't remove the heartache, the misery of what she is, has become, has lost.

She sometimes cries in the shower.

Yesterday evening was a shower night. I had rinsed most of the soap from her calves and feet – I work from top to bottom, as a rule – when she started to wail, a high-pitched keening sound that tore at my heart. I couldn't think what the matter was. The water wasn't too hot or too cold. I had her securely in my arms. She wasn't at risk of falling.

'What's wrong, my love? What's happened to you? It's not like you to make that sort of noise.'

I could see that she was trying to stop and the crying was now more of a whimper. She was doing her best to speak, fighting to get the words out.

'What if…' Her breathing short. 'Collapse. In night?'

'I'll be there to help you.'

'You upstairs. Won't hear.'

She was evidently very much upset by the possibility of being abandoned, left alone, sprawled on the carpet, a part of her broken perhaps.

'I'll be there, sweetheart. Don't worry. You've got your alarm, remember? All you have to do is push the button and it'll ring in my bedroom. I'll keep it right next to me. By my pillow. You're safe, my darling.'

That appeared to ease her mind, but then, minutes later, she began to choke, doubtless brought on by her distress. Her eyes watered up. She couldn't speak.

'Try to cough, my darling. It will help.'

I could see she was gagging. Whether it was in response to the coughing or my suggestion, it was impossible to tell. I fetched water from the kitchen, made her take sips. Gradually, the choking subsided.

'You frightened me there! We can't have you having these fits. I think we'll talk to the clinic, see if we can get anything to help.'

She smiled, appreciated that a plan of action was always preferable to mere compassion.

I dried her with an expensive towel I'd just bought in John

Lewis, gentler on her skin, wrapping her in soft warmth.

'You kind,' she said.

I kissed the top of her head and kissed her shoulder and wondered whether I might just melt in tears right then. But I had to be strong, had to keep on. I breathed deeply and held back and took her in my arms and helped her to her bed in the sitting room. She sat on the edge of the mattress, naked, shivering a little, the towel damp on the floor. I lifted her nightdress over her head and stretched it down over her breasts and stomach. I slid my arms under hers and raised her to standing while the nightdress fell to her knees.

'Do you need the toilet?'

'Alright,' she said.

I sat her down and she folded sideways.

'Stay?' she asked.

'Of course, sweetheart, if that's what you want.'

How much longer can we continue like this? It has reached a point at which I do essentially everything for her. I feed her, clothe her, wash her, brush her teeth. When she visits the toilet, I carry her there and wait and clean her afterwards.

How much longer?

'You don't have to bear this for my sake,' I said. 'You know that.'

'Know.'

'We've joked about The Swiss Option, but it's there to take, if you want to. It is a choice, Kim, and I'm not sure you want to suffer this horrible disease to its bitter conclusion.'

'May....be.'

'How will we make the decision?'

She did not immediately reply, then:

'We?'

It was a figure of speech. For me. Of course, it would and must be Kim who decides. But I suspected she'd taken what I'd said the wrong way. Did she think that I wanted her to die?

'I didn't mean we. You will make your own decision. But *we* should discuss it, don't you think?'

'Lift me.'

She wanted to sit up, to be helped from the bed and into an armchair. It was her way of telling me that if we were to have a conversation about how she would die, she couldn't do it lying down, on the bridge of sleep.

'Drink.'

'Tea?'

'Whis.....ky.'

Insistent. Another signal that we were to talk in a different register. I fetched tumblers, the decanter, ice, poured her what I thought was a decent measure. She raised her better hand, palm upwards. I added a further splash of the malt. She took it from me and stared at it.

'Ore ice.'

Whisky isn't good for Kim. It soothes her sore throat, but at the same time it relaxes muscles that are already weak and beginning to atrophy. That is why she shakes. Her throat has lost its vigour. It no longer coordinates her breathing and swallowing as it should. The whisky will, if anything, promote choking. And then what?

But how can I refuse her one of her very few pleasures?

'I don't think we can any longer discuss this in the abstract, can we? I mean, I've read about all the failed attempts to legalise assisted dying. I know there's a 'slippery slope' argument. But that's not what we're about, is it?'

She said no. She drank, methodically.

'It's a question of whether you've had enough, my darling.'

'Know that. Gary.'

She does this whenever I broach the subject. She makes me feel as if I'm pushing the agenda, pushing her towards it, but that's not the case. There will come a time, in the not too distant future, when Kim is quite unable to speak. I want to know what her view of The Swiss Option is ahead of that. Yes, she may be able to communicate by other means, even then, alphabet boards, texts, a digital voice, and so on, but those will be no substitute for the nuanced clarity of speech.

'You right,' she said. 'I don't to suffer the end. But how know when?'

50

KIM

8th February 2018

It's painfully slow to write, but I must, for as long as my hand lasts.

A speech and language therapist called today. She gave me some exercises that are designed to dilate my airway so that I can swallow more easily and speak in a way that Gary can understand. He tries to hear me, but my God, I have to repeat myself over and over! It's exhausting.

Note to self: I must investigate the voice recording service Paddy talked about at the care centre.

Did I give Gary the wrong impression? About The Swiss Option? I can't remember what I said. Memories are fading these days. I want to put them down, but I'm finding it so much harder to write. I used the alphabet board for the first time the other day. It was easier to move letters around with the tip of my finger than to write the words with a pen. I liked the look of them, large red letters on a yellow background.

They said: FRESH AIR.

He only took me around the block. The air was mild, a light breeze, and I loved the warmth of the sun as it landed on my face and hands. It seemed like an act of divine kindness.

We met the Dobbs in Park Avenue. They clearly find the sight of me lolling in my chair uncomfortable so the conversation was short and they were eager to get away. I watched them as they crossed the road and headed towards town. I felt they were on the verge of breaking into a run.

Did I say that I wanted to go ahead with The Swiss Option?

Do I?

So far, I have been writing for twenty minutes. It's slow, partly because of my shaky hand, but also because I grapple with the words. Others rush in and obscure the ones I want.

Memory, too, plays tricks these days. I jumble up the Highlands and Le Touquet, South Africa and that little village we went to in Sussex with the large church. It was a cinque port. That much I know. Why can I remember that detail and not the name of the place? It's frustrating. Gary tries to put it down to age rather than MND. I'm only forty-five, for God's sake. He's being kind, of course.

I find it difficult to distinguish memory and dream. I often wake up in the past. As I open my eyes, I realise I've been elsewhere, oceans away, and I believe I've had memories of events, things Gary and I have done together. They seem to have the solidity of fact, of lived experience.

But they may be dreams. Probably are.

They console me. All of me is deteriorating, including memory itself. (Have I written that already?) These waking thoughts, rushing in soon after dawn, are precious. They are vivid and everyone I see is healthy and robust and agile.

This morning it was just Gary and me, on a hot summer afternoon. It must have been lunchtime. We are sitting on the bank of a burn. I can feel the warmth of the grass under me. Gary is unpacking sandwiches, smoked trout, from silver foil. I have the job of snapping the caps off beer bottles. One of them leaps from my hand into the fast burn, catching the silver light as it's swept away. It makes me laugh, then and now, my collapsed lopsided laugh no one should be obliged to see. But *then*? A burst of joy!

Gary always loved my laughter. We always enjoyed a laugh, laughing together.

How good the trout tastes, the malted bread, the chilled beer. I can recover the tastes if I try. Strange that I can taste things I remember, but not the things I eat and drink every day. It seems that, even as I fall apart, the past, or at least the past I see in my dreams, intensifies.

Out there by the burn, sandwiches over, we tighten our bootlaces and stand up and climb the gorse hill above us and the sun shines hot and my face burns and the burn glistens and Gary takes my hand and there is no motor neurone disease and birds fly, their wings unbroken, and we are happy amidst a cloudless sky.

51

GARY

November 2018

I have been out since late afternoon. First, I wanted to test the tyre pressures on the Hilux, something I've been meaning to do for weeks. I drove over to Fraser's. The garage was closed, but the airline was working. I didn't think he'd mind if I made use of it.

Then I popped into Angus's store to pick up ingredients for this evening's meal. He was in his usual mischievous mood.

'Your friend is staying on a few days?'

'Sally? Yes. Just until the end of the week, I think. I don't know her well.'

'You said that.'

'More of a friend of my wife. Cycling companion.'

'Yes.'

He knows all this. Why do I feel the need to repeat everything, to explain not only Sally's presence but the relationship I have to her? It was so much easier to account for myself alone.

'I saw what they'd done to your memorial,' Angus remarks.

'Who on earth?'

'Are you of the view it's mere vandalism?'

'I don't know what to make of it.'

He wants to speak further and scans the barcodes of my items painstakingly, lobbing them, one by one, into a carrier bag hung on metal arms. A packet of steak, broccoli, four potatoes, butter times two, washing up liquid, shaving gel. They thud into the carrier.

'It could, mind you, be a message intended for yourself, Mr Montrose.'

'That's a possibility, of course. As I say, I'm at a loss.'

'What would it be about?'

'We Know What You Did?'

'And the rest.'

I give him cash to pay and he hands me the carrier.

'The rest?'

'You should report it to the police. WPC Culley. Hannah. She's your woman.'

I hurry out of the shop. The rest? What did Angus mean? There is still enough light to drive up and take a look. I text Sally to say I'll be late home.

It takes me twenty minutes or so to reach the knoll. I park up below and start to walk up the hill. The sun has already shrunk away and the ladder hangs above me in a grey gloom, soon to fade, hints of a sea mist developing beyond the beach.

I climb the *cnocan*, low-spirited, uncertain what I'm about to find. The ladder looks strikingly different in this dim dusk. Robbed of its sheen, it has a melancholy, as perhaps a memorial to the deceased should. I don't know. I'd always thought of it as a celebration, of colour and light, the twin pulses of your life, my love. Today, it stands like the marker of a grave, no less compelling, but drawing the visitor, those who look on, to a place not of the living, but the dead.

I suppose Angus's words have prepared me, but it's nonetheless a shock. The first slogan, WE KNOW WHAT YOU

DID, stands at head height, untidily spelt out in a matt white paint. But there is a second, lower down, neater, this time in red. There is anger in it, *fearg*.

It says *THOU SHALT NOT KILL.*

52

GARY

February 2018

I came down earlier than usual this morning to find Kim awake and anxious. It was awful to see. She couldn't speak. I watched her for what seemed like minutes at a time, but was probably mere seconds. Her lips made flitting movements. She was struggling to get her tongue to work, to make speech. Instead, she produced noises, whines and groans, noises of distress in different registers, some high and hysterical, others deep like grief.

I tried to understand her, but it was impossible. I wanted to hug her, kiss her, reassure her.

She stank of her own excrement. She must have soiled herself in the night. Why didn't she use the alarm? Her muscles are so weak she might well not have felt anything, but she must surely have been aware of the smell. Perhaps the alarm failed. I must test it. Or had I drunk too much to hear it?

She couldn't have called out, thwarted by her delinquent tongue. I held her limp hands, squeezed gently, as if to say 'I love you. How awful this is for you!' but not quite mustering the words, all of it implicit in my eyes, my hands, all the love, all the awfulness, the sadness, the damnation.

The tears crawled down her cheeks, shining misery. I lifted her in my arms, her weight dead as ever, but less of it. She has lost over a stone in the last month. I carried her, weeping, her arms clinging around my neck, her eyes full of needless apology. I tried to do this as quickly as possible, but she was embarrassed, by her stained nightdress, by the dried excrement on her thighs and arse, the stench. She made feeble movements with her better hand, as if she wanted to bat me away.

'It's alright,' I said. 'There's no shame. Let's just get you cleaned up.'

I used the hand shower, gentler I thought than the overhead, and methodically sponged her, cleaning away the dirt, restoring her to how she wanted to be, decent.

'There. You see! No time at all. You've scrubbed up nicely.'

She cried again, few tears, but her shoulders were lifted and shaking like a frightened child.

I dried her poor body and held her close for several minutes.

Is this what the future holds for us? Unavoidable and repeated humiliation for Kim; the duty that has no end for me, the failure to console or heal?

How much of it can she bear, can either of us bear? Is this what you want, my love, or has the time come, the time we've expected all along and dreaded, the time for us to part?

53

KIM

27th February 2018

Will this be my last entry? My right hand has gone the way of the left. It has so little strength in it. I fight to hold on to the pen and make the letters and words. Keeping my head upright is an ordeal too, which adds to the difficulty of writing.

I will try to write again, though, because this and the alphabet board are the only remaining ways for me to communicate. My tongue seems to float in my mouth. Occasionally, I can find the shape of a word, but mostly I mutter and groan.

Please God, there isn't much more.

I saw Adrianna last night, in a dream of so much joy and beauty that I woke up having forgotten I had this disease and it was such a cruel shock to realise the truth.

Adrianna had grown up into a young woman. She was wearing a fascinator, emerald green, twisted into a large flower with petals of fine green net. In the dream, it hangs over one side of her face. We hold hands, grip hands, grip the white fence that separates us from the racecourse. We're excited, shouting. *Indomabile! Indomabile!* Our horse, our Italian horse, the horse we always back, last seen winning at the Capannelle in Rome. He's winning here! The thunder of hooves, the scream of the crowd with their arms flung high, we can scarcely hear each other speak. She is beautiful, my daughter.

I wish she had been.

I can no longer cry. I well up. Tears form in the ducts, but I have no strength and they can't fall. You need strength to cry.

So they say.

54

GARY

November 2018

'He's right, Angus, about the police,' Sally says. 'That's exactly what you should be doing. It's not a big island. Someone's bound to know who bloody did it. He's probably got form. The police should find him in a jiffy.'

'Him?'

'Don't you think? It's got to be a man, I reckon.'

'I've no idea. If you say so.'

'I just think it's aggressive. It's a threat, isn't it? I don't understand how it's supposed to work, but it's like the guy who did it wants you to know he has a secret you share. Don't you think? A woman would go about it differently.'

'He says *we. We* Know What You Did.'

'Yes, that's weird, isn't it? Perhaps it's meant to be intimidating. What do you think he knows about you?'

'Can't imagine.'

I can, of course. Imagine. It is all too easy to allow myself to speculate, to scrutinise all the encounters I have had and the memories I've given away. Who knows what's been made of them? I have no evidence, nothing to present to WPC Curren, Hannah, but I have rising intuitions, fears that I have somehow antagonised or even threatened someone.

'I've been going through Kim's diary.'

What! Utter shock, a numbing fact. When I respond, it seems to me delayed, as if I'd hesitated, didn't know what to say or was slow to understand.

'You did what! That's a bit bloody inappropriate, don't you think? Fuck! What the hell did you think you were doing?'

'She was a friend. I don't think she'd mind.'

'No? For fuck's sake! No, I don't think so!'

I'm furious, astonished by her presumption. What makes her think she can pry into someone's privacy, Kim's, so unashamedly?

'As far as I know, you weren't close friends. You've no bloody business reading it!'

'We got to know each other pretty well, actually, Gary. On cycle rides and so on. You weren't there!'

'You shouldn't have read it. You had no right. Fuck! I think you should leave.'

She makes no effort to move.

'What are you doing here, anyway? You turn up at Kim's memorial. Out of the bloody blue! Just a coincidence, was it? I don't think so.'

'Don't be ridiculous, Gary!'

'Really? Ridiculous, am I? You didn't come here to snoop? Did you actually have a wedding to go to?'

'Yes.' She said it quietly, added 'Of course.'

Even in my anger, I'm struck by her coolness, her poise. It's as if she is determined to be patient with me.

'How did you find it?' I demand.

She doesn't answer. To my surprise, she produces the diary. She has kept it beside her, jammed between a cushion and the arm of the sofa. She appears to read an entry, too far from me to know when it was made. The sight of Kim's handwriting, not seen for so many months, chokes me for a moment. When I speak, I squawk.

'You shouldn't have bloody touched it. It was hers. Her private life.'

'Get over it, Gary. Please. There are important things in it, things you and I should discuss. Kim wouldn't have cared about me dipping into her diary. I knew her. She wouldn't mind.'

Wouldn't she? Don't I mind? Don't I have any say?

'My God! She went through it, didn't she? And you, of course. But not so much. Not in the way she did. Sorry! That's badly put. You know what I mean.'

Dipping into it! Do you hear this, my love? All those thoughts and feelings you committed to paper in the last months, the last days: for whom were you writing? Me? Yourself? Certainly not Sally! I haven't read your diary for a while, so I can't quite remember what you said. Do I have to worry, now that Sally has read it? Did you implicate me?

'You discussed assisted dying,' Sally says.

We are in the sitting room. She sits opposite me. The room is cold. I have the heating on, but it's not sufficient for an island winter.

'I'll light the burner.'

I keep a good stack of logs in a wicker basket next to the stove.

'She refers to it as The Swiss Option. It's like you can't bring yourselves to call a spade a spade. Why can't you say 'assisted dying'? Or, God forbid, 'assisted suicide'?'

'It was our way of handling it.'

'Was she in favour?'

Four logs will do. For the moment. I've set a bed of paper and kindling, the logs on top of them. What have I done with the gas firelighter I usually keep with the logs? Of course! I used it in the kitchen.

She grabs my hand as I'm leaving the sitting room.

'She seems a bit ambivalent.'

I open drawers in the Welsh dresser, try to locate the firelighter. Gusts of wind and rain slap against the kitchen window. There is rainwater on the sill. The day is bitter now, losing light, closing down. Ahead, I envisage an evening restless with anxiety, even panic. Can I face it, going back into that room, going over it all, enduring her endless questions? She is stumbling her way towards the inevitable. As yet, she is blind, hands stretched out in front of her, feeling her way. But she will get there. She will reach a conclusion eventually, *the* conclusion.

'Sit next to me,' she says.

I hesitate, open the wood stove doors.

'This should warm us up.'

She smiles. It is a peculiar smile. I sense that it's oddly conspiratorial, as if we were engaged in something, some project or secret, together. I ignite the firelighter and stab it in amongst the kindling. It takes immediately. I feel the surge of warmth in my face and hands. The blaze is like sunshine, burst from a cloud. It has taken me less than a minute to light the burner, a trivial delay. I shut the stove doors, turn to Sally.

'Do you remember what she wrote?' she asks.

'Some parts more than others. It could be pretty mundane.'

'Of course. No, I meant on the subject of assisted dying. There's a bit in February. Where is it?'

She flicks through the pages in a hurry, as though there were a deadline by which she must present her evidence.

'Here we are. 8th February. Remember?'

'I– '

'No, you can't possibly. I'll remind you. This is what she says. *Did I give Gary the wrong impression? About The Swiss Option? I can't remember what I said.* And then later she writes: *Did I say I wanted to go ahead with The Swiss Option? Do I?* That doesn't exactly sound committed to it, does it?'

'True, but there are other entries that are different.'

'Are there? I couldn't find any.'

'If you read carefully.'

'I must have missed them, then. I'm sorry. Do you mind talking about this? Is it very distressing?'

'A little.'

'I just want to get to the bottom of it.'

'The bottom of what?'

'What she really thought about assisted dying?'

'What does it matter to you?'

'Have you forgotten?'

Forgotten what? I'm amazed by her self-importance. She was Kim's friend, yes, but they weren't close. They cycled together. That was it, as far as I know. They might have chatted a bit on their bike rides, had a drink in the pub afterwards. I don't recall there being any intimacy.

'I'm sorry?'

'You've forgotten. My charity, silly. The hospice where I work now. It's one of the subjects we're constantly arguing about. Is there a legal framework that could make it safe and foolproof?'

It's as if I took a wrong turning into a dangerous housing estate. I've been afraid my car will stall, that I'll be carjacked or worse. The anxiety is unimaginable, running wild. But then I turn a corner. There are traffic lights ahead, the main road. They turn green. I settle into second gear and coast my way – it seems silently – to freedom, into the stream of cars heading into the City. I'm immediately aware of the adrenaline that has coursed through me. But I'm free, out of harm's way.

'Would you like a whisky?'

'No,' she says. 'I'm happy as we are.'

She sidles up to me, slips her arm through mine, leans her head into my shoulder.

'Kim could never remember what I did for a living either.'

'Her memory collapsed towards the end.'

'Oh, I don't mean then. I didn't know her then. Earlier, before her illness. You two always gave the impression that you were so involved with each other, you had no time for outsiders.'

Did we?

55

GARY

1st March 2018

A reflexologist has visited us today, a tall chatty woman in white trainers and purple lipstick. She greets me like a long-lost friend, but I swear I've never seen her.

'And how's our Kim getting along?'

She says it as she enters the room where Kim is reclining in her electric chair with the adjustable back. Kim isn't particularly aware of her, too much in her own world. Saliva slips down her chin and she is trying to make her good hand clean it away. It's too painful to watch. I step across the room and dry her with a tissue.

'How are you, Kim?' the reflexologist asks. 'Keeping up your spirits?'

Kim stares, blind to her visitor's presence, conscious of language spoken and not understood. I know the signs. She is struggling for some shred of identity, to wake up and be the person she vaguely remembers. But it's impossible and hopeless.

'I'm Beth, Kim. I'm going to do your feet, dear. Might make you feel a bit better. Alright?'

Beth kneels in front of my broken wife and begins to remove her slippers and socks. I wash Kim in the shower two or three times a week. I know her body as intimately as a husband can, but this morning I see her feet for what they are, as others see them: pallid, shrunken and useless, the toenails dark, the toes buckled. She has all but gone, my poor wife, left me to another future.

'Are you feeling that, my darling?' Beth asks. 'Are they numb? Let's see if we can put some feeling back.'

She presses, strokes, pushes the misshapen toes back from the pad of the foot, manipulates the ankles. Kim makes noises, but even I can't tell if they are groans of pleasure or of pain. Beth seems to think she *can* tell.

'There, that's good. It's a nice feeling, isn't it?'

Beth is with us for an hour. Whether or not there is any point in this kind of treatment I can't decide. If I'm honest, I was a sceptic when it came to Reflexology long before Kim's illness. I hesitated to give it a capital 'R'. But thousands swear by it, don't they? I shouldn't dismiss it out of hand. It's simply that I'm convinced Kim is beyond therapy, beyond repair.

'Does she seem reasonably content in herself?' Beth asks, as she's leaving.

'Not really. I think she's miserable every fucking minute of every day. Except when she's asleep.'

'It can't be a bad as all that.'

'Why not? I'm sure she'd rather be dead.'

'Now, now, we can't have talk like that, Gary. Anyway, look after her, won't you? I'll be back next month.'

I suppose that's how these saintly carers cope. They come into people's homes, they minister to the damned and dying, observe their sickness and their suffering, conscious that all hope for them has long since shattered. So they put their energy into a charade of solicitude, something better than nothing, a show of kindness, faultless to the last.

I admire these people. I respect them, their work. And yet it makes me unspeakably angry. I can't bear the sham of it.

Kim needs water. I fetch the beaker and gently feed the straw between her dry lips. I remind myself that I must put moisturiser on them, lip salve. If I raise the beaker a fraction, the water passes up the straw and slips into her mouth without overwhelming or challenging her too much. She chokes so readily these days. I'm always on the watch for it, and I keep the amounts of food and drink she swallows to the minimum required.

'There you go, my love. Not so parched now. I should have noticed earlier.'

Is there gratitude in those eyes, even affection? I think so. Her mouth moves erratically. It's as if she's trembling. Her lips part, and saliva rolls on to her chin. I dab it away, kiss her forehead. Her eyes look painfully vulnerable, perhaps fearful. What is the salvation she wants in that moment? Does she want me to protect her or deliver her from this agony?

Would God know? If He cared.

56

GARY

November 2018

I explained to Sally that it was too soon. It's not a year since Kim died. I can't contemplate a relationship with another woman just yet. She withdrew her hand and gradually moved away from me. She didn't appear upset by my rejection.

'Maybe later,' she said, simply.

Frankly, I don't think it likely. Sally is not really my type. No one is my *type*, of course, because I'm permeated by memories of Kim, of our shared experiences, our harnessed view of the world, our misery. They preclude any possibility of other intimacy. Kim was, and is, all.

I'd had enough of this.

'Shall we go out? Find a pub? I don't really fancy cooking tonight.'

'But it's so cosy in here.'

'Just for an hour or so.'

Outside, it had begun to freeze. There was ice on the windscreen of the Hilux and I had to labour at it with a credit card I borrowed from Sally. She was puzzled that I appeared not to have one of my own.

I wound up the heat in the cab, flannelled away the condensation and we drove in silence to a pub on the south side of the island, The Drovers, an eighteenth century inn with its original beams in the ceiling and, thankfully, no music.

We sat on stools at a round table in the window. I had whisky, Sally a large glass of red wine. There weren't many people in that night, three men chatting to the barman in Gaelic, a couple by the log fire. I thought it might be too quiet for what I had to say. But the fire was spitting, the men at the bar were making each other laugh and, whenever anyone crossed the room to stack the fire or visit the toilet, the floorboards creaked.

Our conversation would not be overheard.

'I don't know what you think happened when Kim was dying, but I can assure you– '

'I want to know if you helped her die.'

'You're asking me that here?'

'Is that why we've come out? So I can't ask you? You can trust me.'

Really?

'I need another drink. Shall I order food while I'm up there?'

'No, hang on!'

I'd left the table and she wasn't going to shout after me. The barman came over and I asked for another double. I couldn't look at Sally and I pretended to be absorbed in the evening meal menu chalked onto a board behind the bar.

I went back to our table.

'They have Steak & Guinness Pie, haggis and neeps, fish and chips, lasagne and a venison casserole.'

'Nothing vegetarian?'

'Sorry, yes, there's vegetarian bangers and mash, oh and also a veggie burger.'

'That'll do me, please.' She smiled. 'You're going to have to give me an answer.'

'I know.'

I gave the barman our order and returned to Sally.

'Well?'

It interested me that she wasn't more earnest, more serious. If anything, she appeared amused by our conversation. Perhaps she enjoyed putting me on the spot, watching me dance on the head of a pin.

'All adds up, you know,' she said. 'Coming up here. Changing your name. Did you *help* her?'

'I suppose it depends on what you mean by *help*?'

'Don't bloody wriggle, Gary! It doesn't suit you. Did you or didn't you? I'm not going to tell anyone.'

'In a strict sense?'

'Whatever sense you like. Just come out with it. Be honest.'

'If I tell you, what use is it to you?'

'None. Perhaps none. I don't know. I'm not here to judge you.'

'No?'

'No,' she said, firmly.

'Most people do.'

'Really? Like who?'

'Whoever wrote those words on Kim's memorial.'

'He doesn't know anything.'

'How can you be so sure?'

'Have you talked openly to anyone? No? I thought not.'

Our food arrived. It was an opportunity to delay the subject further. I ate my fish and chips slowly, pausing some while between forkfuls, glancing around the pub. Was I reluctant to tell her the truth? Clearly. Was I ashamed, guilty even? I don't believe so. I think my hesitancy concerned the choice of words, the dearth of them, to express what I suspected no one could possibly understand. The physical facts, the biological facts, were crude. They would evoke sympathy, certainly, but not a full appreciation of what Kim had been through, of the brutal future that lay ahead of her in the remaining weeks or months, the desecration of a human body, the pitiful loss of control of movement and function, the chokings and the twitches and the evacuations, the slobber and soiling. All, all, while her mind was almost intact, at times alert enough to the atrocity happening to her, to what was being meted out to her in front of her face, shame beyond excuse or comfort, the deep mortification of her soul. If you couldn't imagine it, if you couldn't inhabit it, then all my actions would appear merely culpable and vile.

'Did you,' she said yet again, 'help her?'

There was manageable risk and there was foolhardiness. I didn't know which it was, but I said, simply, yes.

57

GARY

8th March 2018

The sitting room where she lies is unexpectedly dazzling. Late afternoon sunshine is framed by the garden window and throws a kind of melted geometry onto the wall behind her. This last golden light is being squeezed from the day and it rests softly on the sofa cushions and the tall oak bookcase my mother left us.

Kim is asleep. She has looked composed, serene even, for the past few hours. I won't disturb her. We spoke at length this morning and that was sufficient. Well, I spoke, to be accurate, but I know that she understood. The kindness in her eyes, the occasional tremor of her lips, they intimated her full agreement. I'm sure of that.

She managed to eat the scrambled eggs I cooked for her lunch, then signalled I should prepare her for an afternoon nap. I propped her up on pillows, just enough that she wouldn't have any pain in her shoulders or neck. I took care to wrap her up tightly in the sheet and blanket. She's always anxious these days that she might fall out of bed. She feels secure if I do this.

Is there a chill in the room? I have turned up the electric fire. I want her to be warm. I want her to be comfortable. I think she is. Her breathing is slow and regular, just the occasional cough or gasp, which is as good as it gets.

The sun is sinking, light fading.

I sit beside her for a while, holding her soft hand. Her fingernails are long, painted purple. There has been little we can do about her disfigured feet and toenails, but she likes her hands to look as attractive as weakness allows. She likes me to put moisturiser on them and nail varnish, a new colour each week. Along with the flowers I buy every Friday from a stall outside the train station – I can't face going to the shop now - they are the proofs that colour remains in her reduced life. Friday's flowers always bring a crooked smile to her face that I've come to look forward to.

Don't they, my darling?

I should probably trim her fingernails.

Except that there's little point now.

Her wedding ring slides easily up and down her ring finger. It's a miracle it hasn't fallen off, when I've been manoeuvring her on the toilet, say, or in the shower. If I were a superstitious man, I'd attach significance to that tenacity, but as it is, I think it's luck. God knows, there's little enough of it around.

The last of the sun is blinding me through the garden window, the last gasp, making itself felt. Another day passed. I move a rogue strand of hair from her eyes, pin it behind her ear.

'There, my darling. That's better, isn't it?'

I have loved you, Kim, all my adult life. You know that. We have loved each other for what? Twenty-two years, isn't it? Come May. And here we are. You've been my keel, steadying me. When the boat rolled, I held on to you.

I remember so much. Don't you? Valentine's Day in Le Touquet, when I proposed in Restaurant Perard. Do you remember? I produced your engagement ring and you said no and it seemed to me the whole restaurant fell silent. I don't know what I felt. Embarrassed? It was more shock and hurt, if I'm frank.

I forgave you.

After all, we were back in that same restaurant two days later. We ate oysters and, I think, grilled turbot. Do you remember? And you said 'Ask me again'. So I did. By candlelight. And you said yes that time, and you made me the happiest man in Le Touquet, in France perhaps, the world.

You're all broken, aren't you, sweetheart?

Can you picture us outside that restaurant in St Mark's? Under that bright red canopy? It was such a cold night, pouring with rain. It must have been near midnight. We'd just arrived, and you were so excited, your first visit. The square was almost empty, had it to ourselves. The paving was wet and shining. The stones of Venice. We were happy. For the first time after we'd lost Adrianna. Do you remember?

How could you forget?

We had pizza and Italian beer, and you said to me 'We don't need anyone else, do we?' Or did you say that somewhere else? I can't recall. Perhaps you said it several times. Anyway, it was true, wasn't it? We'd lost Adrianna, but we'd survived. We had each other. Just us.

So, what now, my beautiful wife? What now?

You fought it, didn't you? As best you could. You tried to stay fit. You'd force us out in the Highland rain. You weren't bothered by the cold or the wet. You kept going. But it was a monster, wasn't it? You couldn't defeat it.

It was worth the fight, though, wasn't it?

Are you crying, sweetheart? In your sleep? Your eyes are

watery. Perhaps you can hear me. I don't want to upset you. I'll remind you of better times. Shall I? Or will you cry anyway, hearing about those happy days?

Remember Table Mountain? Oh my God, you did not want to go up in that cable car. I had to ply you with wine before you'd get on to it. It was such a gorgeous sunset, wasn't it, like today's? The colours in the sky, that's what appealed to you. The yellows and purples and pinks and those thin white trails. Never the same, was it? Always changing. A deep coppery glow by the end. We stayed longer than we'd intended. You said something strange. What was it? Oh, I know. You said: *Do you think things will work out for us? In the long run?* What did I say? It was getting quite cold. I thought we ought to go, but you wanted an answer. I said something like that we'd done alright so far. You weren't very happy with that.

But it was true. Is true. We've done alright, haven't we?

I dab away the saliva from her chin, kiss her there. Her skin is moist and soft.

Has the time come, my darling? I shouldn't delay much more.

It's dark now. The light's gone out. I switch on the table lamps. Their light is gentle, spilt on the furnishings. Kim is in semi-darkness, in the penumbra cast by our drinks cabinet and the television that sits on top of it. I go back to her, hold her hand once again.

This is not a time for sad music, is it? I can hear a triumphal march, can't you? A crescendo. Sibelius's Third Symphony perhaps? Or, no, it's that last act of Prokofiev's *Romeo and Juliet.* Because this is the climax, sweetheart, the finale. We are going to end all this for you, all your misery and pain and frustration.

All your inability and humiliation. This is the moment in the song, the moment you were waiting for.

To be free.

We want to stop your suffering, my darling. So, I won't delay any longer.

The room is very warm now. I place the cushion over her face and press down, gently.

Goodbye, my precious darling, my Kim.

There is resistance, the sound of protest muted by the cushion and her weakness. Is there a desperate effort to live, going on beneath my patient hands? I don't know. I can't be sure. I don't believe so. She has no strength, no animal fight. Instead, I feel her going under, slipping away from me, from life.

In a few minutes it is done.

The room is too much, its unvarying silence, the shadows.

I am exhausted, need fresh air.

58

GARY

6th December 2018

Dear Sally

I first thought I'd email you, but then I realised you'd get that too soon. I needed there to be time between me writing this down and you reading it, time for me to put my decision beyond question or reproach, hence a letter.

By now, you will have gathered that I've left the island. Our conversation the other night in the pub, when you asked me whether or not I'd helped Kim to die, made me realise that I can't continue this life of deception, of pretending to be someone I'm not, someone without the past I've had, someone who hasn't done what I have done.

I spent Friday thinking about what to do. I could have discussed it with you, but frankly I didn't want to be swayed by you one way or another. I didn't want you to influence my decision. I wanted it to be mine alone. In the end, after mulling it over all day, I made up my mind to catch last night's ferry. I've left the Hilux, by the way. The keys are on the Welsh dresser. Feel free to use it.

I arrived in Oban in the early hours this morning. It was bucketing down in the harbour, but I was quite soon on a train to Glasgow, and have since picked up a connection to London. I'll get there around midnight.

I don't suppose we'll meet again, Sally. That's a pity, but it's how it has to be. I'd like to thank you for visiting me. I can't say it was easy. You spotted my change of name straightaway, and I found that your curiosity about how Kim died was a constant source of stress. Not your fault at all. You couldn't possibly know how thin the ice was you were treading on. And I should have taken more care to hide Kim's diary. If you hadn't read it, and drawn the conclusion you did, perhaps I wouldn't be on this train today. Perhaps I would have stayed longer.

I don't regret what I've done. The odd thing is that although I'm absolutely certain I did right by Kim, did the right thing for her, I'm overwhelmed by the scale of it, the seriousness of it, as if the answer dwarfed the question.

Or is it that there never was an answer, only a deep, irrefutable question?

There came a point when I could no longer bear to watch her and she could no longer bear to be watched. That's it. Put simply. I won't terrify you with the full details of her decline into near-total paralysis because they were beyond sadness, but I hope you'll trust me when I say that no human being on God's earth should be made to go through them, and to sit by and see it happen felt like collusion, like allowing torture to be carried out in front of my eyes.

People talk about a 'slippery slope'. They fear that once the exceptional case has been condoned, others will follow with symptoms that are less severe, consent less clear. They talk about 'coercion', the fear that, without having a say, the old or vulnerable will be led down the garden path to their own extinction, intimidated into cooperating by greedy relatives, eager to get hold of their houses, their money, their jewels.

Maybe. I don't know. Aren't we bright enough to come up with a formula that works?

In any case, I don't care. I'm not really a proselytiser. I won't be campaigning for assisted dying at the next election. I can only talk about my specific case, Kim's case. When I spoke to Struan Lamont, the two occasions we touched on the subject, he was adamant that the choice to live or to die isn't ours, but God's. Anyway, I was polite, I think, but I wanted to scream to the rafters – or what is it they have on boats? The yardarm? – I'd shout 'What's God got to do with it?' If I learnt anything from Kim's suffering, it was that God played no part in it, or if He did, it was malicious.

It is a dreadful moment when you take another human being's life. Is that act made more or less dire if the human being in question is your wife, your beloved? We held on, you know. We held on for a very long time, for months, hoping that the disease had worked its worst, that the symptoms were now as bad as they would ever be. But the thing about MND is that it's a disease that keeps on giving. There's always something worse around the corner, another loss, another failure to come. It made me appreciate how wonderful we human beings usually are, how versatile and dextrous, how multiple our abilities. You recognize this when, one by one, you see someone lose all of them. All the skills, all the uses: they simply shut down.

I miss her, desperately. But if you say 'Well, if you miss her, why bring about her death? Why didn't you let her continue to live?', I can only say that that would have been selfish. In any case, the Kim I miss is not the woman lying in the sitting room late that afternoon, supine, feeble, twitching. She is another woman altogether, full of vigour, striding a purple heath in the Highlands, laughing about the bogwater that's filled her boots, shouting out her happiness in the Gaelic rain, brimming with life.

So, Sally, I must, as they say, face the music. I cannot be my own judge and jury any longer. If what I have done has any moral justification, others will, I hope, now acknowledge it. My own verdict is insufficient. I cannot look in the mirror and see only blood.

The time has come. For me and for my Kim, my broken wing. The moment has arisen.

Your friend, Gary.

ACKNOWLEDGEMENTS

The lines quoted in Chapter 12 are from The Beatles' song 'Blackbird'.

Many thanks to James Essinger and Zoe Vernon at The Conrad Press for all their help with the publication and promotion of this book; and to Charlotte Mouncey for her excellent cover design.

Huge thanks, too, to all those who read the novel and gave me very useful comments: Joan Bakewell, Simon Berthon, David Crane, John Hudson, Martin and Helen Hughes, Richard Morris, Julia Neuberger, and my loyal children, Tom Waterhouse and Gennie Waterhouse.

And, once again, for their continuing support and advice, my deep gratitude to Richard Kerridge and my wonderful wife, Tessa.

